BY JOAN DIDION

DEMO

A NOVEL BY JOAN

CRACY

DIDION

SIMON AND SCHUSTER / NEW YORK

Copyright © 1984 by Joan Didion
All rights reserved
including the right of reproduction
in whole or in part in any form
Published by Simon and Schuster
A Division of Simon & Schuster, Inc.
Simon & Schuster Building
Rockefeller Center
1230 Avenue of the Americas
New York, New York 10020
SIMON AND SCHUSTER and colophon are
registered trademarks of Simon & Schuster, Inc.
Designed by Edith Fowler
Manufactured in the United States of America

10   9   8   7   6   5   4   3   2   1

Library of Congress Cataloging in Publication Data
Didion, Joan.
* Democracy.*

* I. Title.*
PS3554.I33D4   1984   813'.54   84-1216
ISBN 0-671-41977-3

The author gratefully acknowledges permission to include excerpts from the following works:
* Random Harvest by James Hilton, copyright 1943 by James Hilton. Published by Little, Brown and Company in association with The Atlantic Monthly Press.*
* "Of Mere Being" by Wallace Stevens, copyright © 1957 by Elsie Stevens and Holly Stevens. Reprinted from Opus Posthumous by Wallace Stevens, by permission of Alfred A. Knopf, Inc.*
* "September 1, 1939" by W. H. Auden, copyright 1940 by W. H. Auden. Reprinted from The English Auden by W. H. Auden, edited by Edward Mendelson, by permission of Random House, Inc.*

This book is for Dominique and Quintana.
It is also for Elsie Giorgi.

ONE

1

THE light at dawn during those Pacific tests was something to see.

Something to behold.

Something that could almost make you think you saw God, he said.

He said to her.

Jack Lovett said to Inez Victor.

Inez Victor who was born Inez Christian.

He said: the sky was this pink no painter could approximate, one of the detonation theorists used to try, a pretty fair Sunday painter, he never got it. Just never captured it, never came close. The sky was this pink and the air was wet from the night rain, soft and wet and smelling like flowers, smelling like those flowers you used to pin in your hair when you drove out to Schofield, gardenias, the air in the morning smelled like gardenias, never mind there were not too many flowers around those shot islands.

They were just atolls, most of them.

Sand spits, actually.

Two Quonsets and one of those landing strips they roll down, you know, the matting, just roll it down like a goddamn bathmat.

It was kind of a Swiss Family Robinson deal down

there, really. None of the observers would fly down until the technical guys had the shot set up, that's all I was, an observer. Along for the ride. There for the show. You know me. Sometimes we'd get down there and the weather could go off and we'd wait days, just sit around cracking coconuts, there was one particular event at Johnston where it took three weeks to satisfy the weather people.

Wonder Woman Two, that shot was.

I remember I told you I was in Manila.

I remember I brought you some little souvenir from Manila, actually I bought it on Johnston off a reconnaissance pilot who'd flown in from Clark.

Three weeks sitting around goddamn Johnston Island waiting for the weather and then no yield to speak of.

Meanwhile we lived in the water.

Caught lobsters and boiled them on the beach.

Played gin and slapped mosquitoes.

Couldn't walk. No place to walk. Couldn't write anything down, the point of the pen would go right through the paper, one thing you got to understand down there was why not much got written down on those islands.

What you could do was, you could talk. You got to hear everybody's personal life story down there, believe me, you're sitting on an island a mile and a half long and most of that is the landing strip.

Those technical guys, some of them had been down there three months.

Got pretty raunchy, believe me.

Then the weather people would give the go and bingo, no more stories. Everybody would climb on a transport around three A.M. and go out a few miles and watch for first light.

Watch for pink sky.

And then the shot, naturally.

Nevada, the Aleutians, those events were another situation altogether.

Nobody had very pleasurable feelings about Nevada, although some humorous things did happen there at Mercury, like the time a Livermore device fizzled and the Los Alamos photographers started snapping away at that Livermore tower—still standing, you understand, a two-meg gadget and the tower's still standing, which was the humorous part—and laughing like hell. The Aleutians were just dog duty, ass end of the universe, they give the world an enema they stick it in at Amchitka. Those shots up there did a job because by then they were using computers instead of analog for the diagnostics, but you would never recall an Aleutian event with any nostalgia whatsoever, nothing even humorous, you got a lot of congressmen up there with believe it or not their wives and daughters, big deal for the civilians but zero interest, zip, none.

He said to her.

Jack Lovett said to Inez Victor (who was born Inez Christian) in the spring of 1975.

But those events in the Pacific, Jack Lovett said.

Those shots around 1952, 1953.

Christ they were sweet.

You were still a little kid in high school when I was going down there, you were pinning flowers in your hair and driving out to Schofield, crazy little girl with island fever, I should have been put in jail. I'm surprised your Uncle Dwight didn't show up out there with a warrant. I'm surprised the whole goddamn Christian Company wasn't turned out for the lynching.

Water under the bridge.

Long time ago.

You've been around the world a little bit since.

You did all right.

You filled your dance card, you saw the show.

Interesting times.

I told you when I saw you in Jakarta in 1969, you and I had the knack for interesting times.

Jesus Christ, Jakarta.

Ass end of the universe, southern tier.

But I'll tell you one thing about Jakarta in 1969, Jakarta in 1969 beat Bien Hoa in 1969.

"Listen, Inez, get it while you can," Jack Lovett said to Inez Victor in the spring of 1975.

"Listen, Inez, use it or lose it."

"Listen, Inez, *un regard d'adieu*, we used to say in Saigon, last look through the door."

"Oh shit, Inez," Jack Lovett said one night in the spring of 1975, one night outside Honolulu in the spring of 1975, one night in the spring of 1975 when the C-130s and the C-141s were already shuttling between Honolulu and Anderson and Clark and Saigon all night long, thirty-minute turnaround at Tan Son Nhut, touching down and loading and taxiing out on flight idle, bringing out the dependents, bringing out the dealers, bringing out the money, bringing out the pet dogs and the sponsored bar girls and the porcelain elephants: "Oh shit, Inez," Jack Lovett said to Inez Victor, "Harry Victor's wife."

Last look through more than one door.

This is a hard story to tell.

2

C ALL me the author.

Let the reader be introduced to Joan Didion, upon whose character and doings much will depend of whatever interest these pages may have, as she sits at her writing table in her own room in her own house on Welbeck Street.

So Trollope might begin this novel.

I have no unequivocal way of beginning it, although I do have certain things in mind. I have for example these lines from a poem by Wallace Stevens:

> The palm at the end of the mind,
> Beyond the last thought, rises
> In the bronze distance,
> A gold-feathered bird
> Sings in the palm, without human meaning,
> Without human feeling, a foreign song.

Consider that.

I have: "Colors, moisture, heat, enough blue in the air," Inez Victor's fullest explanation of why she stayed on in Kuala Lumpur. Consider that too. I have those pink dawns of which Jack Lovett spoke. I have the dream, recurrent, in which my entire field of vision fills with rainbow, in which I open a door onto a growth of tropical green (I believe this to be a banana grove, the big glossy fronds heavy with rain, but since no bananas are seen on the palms symbolists may relax) and watch the spectrum separate into pure color. Consider any of these things long enough and you will see that they tend to deny the relevance not only of personality but of narrative, which makes them less than ideal images with which to begin a novel, but we go with what we have.

Cards on the table.

I began thinking about Inez Victor and Jack Lovett at a point in my life when I lacked certainty, lacked even that minimum level of ego which all writers recognize as essential to the writing of novels, lacked conviction, lacked patience with the past and interest in memory; lacked faith even in my own technique. A poignant (to me) assignment I came across recently in a textbook for students of composition: *"Didion begins with a rather ironic reference to her immediate reason to write this piece. Try using this ploy as the opening of an essay; you may want to copy the ironic-but-earnest tone of Didion, or you might try making your essay witty. Consider the broader question of the effect of setting: how does Didion use the scene as a rhetorical base? She returns again and again to different details of the scene: where and how and to what effect? Consider, too, Didion's own involvement in the setting: an atmosphere results. How?"*

Water under the bridge.

As Jack Lovett would say.

Water under the bridge and dynamite it behind you.

So I have no leper who comes to the door every morning at seven.

No Tropical Belt Coal Company, no unequivocal lone figure on the crest of the immutable hill.

In fact no immutable hill: as the granddaughter of a geologist I learned early to anticipate the absolute mutability of hills and waterfalls and even islands. When a hill slumps into the ocean I see the order in it. When a 5.2 on the Richter scale wrenches the writing table in my own room in my own house in my own particular Welbeck Street I keep on typing. A hill is a transitional accommodation to stress, and ego may be a similar accommodation. A waterfall is a self-correcting maladjustment of stream to structure, and so, for all I know, is technique. The very island to which Inez Victor returned in the spring of 1975—Oahu, an emergent post-erosional land mass along the Hawaiian Ridge—is a temporary feature, and every rainfall or tremor along the Pacific plates alters its shape and shortens its tenure as Crossroads of the Pacific. In this light it is difficult to maintain definite convictions about what happened down there in the spring of 1975, or before.

In fact I have already abandoned a great deal of what happened before.

Abandoned most of the stories that still dominate table talk down in that part of the world where Inez Victor was born and to which she returned in 1975.

Abandoned for example all stories about definite cases of typhoid contracted on sea voyages lasting the first ten months of 1856.

Abandoned all accounts of iridescence observed on the night sea off the Canaries, of guano rocks sighted southeast of the Falklands, of the billiards room at the old Hotel Estrella del Mar on the Chilean coast, of a particular boiled-beef lunch eaten on Tristan da Cunha in 1859; and of certain legendary poker games played on the Isthmus of Panama in 1860, with the losses and winnings (in gold) of every player.

Abandoned the bereaved widower who drowned himself at landfall.

Scuttled the festivities marking the completion of the first major irrigation ditch on the Nuannu ranch.

Jettisoned in fact those very stories with which most people I know in those islands confirm their place in the larger scheme, their foothold against the swell of the sea, the erosion of the reefs and the drowning of the valley systems and the glittering shallows left when islands vanish. Would it have been Inez Victor's grandmother Cissy or Cissy's best friend Tita Dowdell who wore the Highland Lassie costume to the Children's Ball at the palace in 1892? If Cissy went as the Highland Lassie and Tita Dowdell as the Spanish Dancer (Inez's grandfather definitely went as one of the Peasant Children of All Nationalities, that much was documented, that much Inez and her sister Janet knew from the photograph that hung on the landing of the house on Manoa Road), then how did the Highland Lassie costume end up with the Palace Restoration Committee on loan from Tita Dowdell's daughter-in-law? On the subject of Tita Dowdell's daughter-in-law, did her flat silver come to her through her father's and Inez and Janet's grandfather's mutual Aunt Tru? Was it likely that Aunt Tru's fire opal from the Great Barrier Reef (surrounded by diamond chips) would have been lost down a drain at the Outrigger Canoe Club if Janet or Inez or even their cousin Alice Campbell had been wearing it instead of Tita Dowdell's daughter-in-law? Where were the calabashes Alice Campbell's father got from Judge Thayer? Who had Leilani Thayer's koa settee? When Inez and Janet's mother left Honolulu on the reconditioned *Lurline* and never came back, did she or did she not have the right to take Tru's yellow diamond? These are all important questions down there, suggestive details in the setting, but the setting is for another novel.

3

"Imagine my mother dancing," that novel began, in the first person. The first person was Inez, and was later abandoned in favor of the third:

"Inez imagined her mother dancing.

"Inez remembered her mother dancing.

"Brown-and-white spectator shoes, very smart. High-heeled sandals made of white silk twine, very beautiful. White gardenias in her hair on the beach at Lanikai. A white silk blouse with silver sequins shaped like stars. Shaped like new moons. Shaped like snowflakes. The sentimental things of life as time went by. Dancing under the camouflage net on the lawn at Kaneohe. Blue moon on the Nuannu ranch. Saw her standing alone. She smiled as she danced.

"Inez remembered no such thing.

"Inez remembered the shoes and the sequins like snowflakes but she only imagined her mother dancing, to make clear to herself that the story was one of romantic outline. You will notice that the daughters in romantic stories always remember their mothers dancing, or about to leave for the dance: these dance-bound mothers materialize in the darkened nursery (never a bedroom in these stories, always a 'nursery,' on the English model) in a cloud of perfume, a burst of light off a diamond hair clip. They glance in the mirror. They smile. They do not linger, for this is one of those moments in which the interests of mothers are seen to diverge sharply from the wishes of daughters. These mothers get on with it. These mothers lean for a kiss and leave for the dance. Inez and Janet's mother left, but not for the dance. Inez and Janet's mother left for San Francisco, on the *Lurline*, reconditioned. I specify 'reconditioned' because that was how Carol Christian's departure was characterized for Inez and Janet, as a sudden but compelling opportunity to make the first postwar crossing on the reconditioned *Lurline*. 'Just slightly irresistible,' was the way Carol Christian put it exactly."

What I had there was a study in provincial manners, in the acute tyrannies of class and privilege by which people assert themselves against the tropics; Honolulu during World War Two, martial law, submariners and fliers and a certain investor from Hong Kong with whom Carol Christian was said to drink brandy and Coca-Cola, a local scandal. I was interested more in Carol Christian than in her daughters, interested in the stubborn loneliness she had perfected during her marriage to Paul Christian, interested in her position as an outsider in the islands and in her compensatory yearning to be "talented," not talented at anything in particular but just talented, a state of social grace denied her by the Christians. Carol Christian arrived in Honolulu as a bride in 1934. By 1946 she was sometimes moved so profoundly by the urge for company that she would keep Inez and Janet home from school on the pretext of teaching them how to do their nails. She read novels out loud to them on the beach at Lanikai, popular novels she checked out from the lending library at the drugstore in Kailua. " 'The random years were at an end,' " she would read, her voice rising to signal a dramatic effect, and then she would invent a flourish of her own: " 'Now, they could harvest them.' Look there, *random harvest*, that explains the title, very poetic, a happy ending, *n'est-ce pas?*"

She was attracted to French phrases but knew only the several she had memorized during the semester of junior college in Stockton, California, that constituted her higher education. She was also attracted to happy endings, and located them for Inez and Janet wherever she could: in the Coke float that followed the skinned knee, in the rainbow after the rain, in magazine stories about furlough weddings and fortuitously misdelivered Dear John letters and, not least, in her own romance, which she dated from the day she left Stockton and got a job modeling at I. Magnin in San Francisco. "Eighteen years old and dressed to kill in a Chanel suit, the real McCoy," she would say to Inez and Janet. Eighteen years old and dressed to kill in a Mainbocher evening pajama, the genuine article. Eighteen years old and dressed to kill in a Patou tea gown, white satin cut on the bias, talk about drop dead, bare to *here* in back. The bias-cut Patou tea gown figured large in Carol Christian's stories because this was the dress in which she had been sneaking a cigarette on the I. Magnin employees' floor when Paul Christian stepped off the elevator by mistake (another fortuitous misdelivery) and brushed the shadows away, brought her happiest day, one look at him and she had found a world completely new, the sole peculiarity being that the world was an island in the middle of the Pacific and Paul Christian was rarely there. "When a man stays away from a woman it means he wants to keep their love alive," Carol Christian advised Inez and Janet. She had an entire codex of these signals men and women supposedly sent to one another (when a woman blew smoke at a man it meant she was definitely interested, and when a man told a woman her dress was too revealing it meant he adored her), dreamy axioms she had heard or read or invented as a schoolgirl of romantic tendency and to which she clung in the face of considerable contrary evidence. That she had miscalculated when she married Paul Christian was a conclusion she seemed incapable of drawing. She made a love-knot of what she imagined to be her first gray hair and mailed it to him in Cuernavaca. "*Mon cher* Paul," she wrote on the card to which she pinned the love-knot. Inez watched her tie the hair but did not see the card for some years, loose in one of the boxes of shed belongings that Paul Christian would periodically ship express collect from wherever he was to Inez and Janet. "Who do you f—— to get off this island? (Just kidding of course) XXXX, C."

She left dark red lipstick marks on her cigarettes,

smoked barely at all and then crushed out in coffee cups and Coke bottles and in the sand. She sat for hours at her dressing table, which was covered with the little paper parasols that came in drinks, yellow, turquoise, shocking pink, tissue parasols like a swarm of brittle butterflies. She sat at this dressing table and shaved her legs. She sat at this dressing table and smoothed Vaseline into her eyebrows. She sat at this dressing table and instructed her daughters in what she construed to be the language of love, a course she had notably failed. For a year or two after Carol Christian left Honolulu Janet would sit on the beach at Lanikai and sift the sand looking for cigarettes stained with her mother's lipstick. She kept the few she found in a shoebox, along with the tissue parasols from Carol Christian's dressing table and the postcards from San Francisco and Carmel and Lake Tahoe.

Of the daughters I was at first more interested in Janet, who was the younger, than in Inez. I was interested in the mark the mother had left on Janet, in Janet's defensive veneer of provincial gentility, her startling and avid preoccupation with other people's sexual arrangements; in her mercantile approach to emotional transactions, and her condescension to anyone less marketable than she perceived herself to be. As an adolescent Janet had always condescended, for example, to Inez, and became bewildered and rather sulky when it worked out, in her view, so well for Inez and so disappointingly for herself. I was interested in how Janet's husband Dick Ziegler made a modest fortune in Hong Kong housing and lost it in the development of windward Oahu. I was interested in Inez and Janet's grandmother, the late Sybil "Cissy" Christian, a woman remembered in Honolulu for the vehement whims and irritations that passed in that part of the world as opinions, as well as for the dispatch with which she had divested herself of her daughter-in-law. *Aloha oe.* "I believe your mother wants to go to night clubs," Cissy Christian said to Inez and Janet by way of explaining Carol Christian's departure. "But she's coming back," Janet said. "Now and then," Cissy Christian said. This conversation took place at lunch at the Pacific Club, one hour after Inez and Janet and their uncle Dwight saw the reconditioned *Lurline* sail. Janet bolted from the table. "Happy now?" Dwight Christian asked his mother. "Somebody had to do it," Cissy Christian said. "Not necessarily before lunch," Dwight Christian said.

I saw it as a family in which the colonial impulse had marked every member. I was interested in Inez and Janet's father, Paul Christian, and in the way in which he had reinvented himself as a romantic outcast, a remittance man of the Pacific. "He's going to end up a goddamn cargo cult," Paul Christian's brother Dwight once said about him. I was interested not only in Paul but in Dwight Christian, in his construction contracts at Long Binh and Cam Ranh Bay, his claim to have played every Robert Trent Jones golf course in the world with the exception of the Royal in Rabat; the particular way in which he used Wendell Omura to squeeze Dick Ziegler out of windward Oahu and coincidentally out of the container business. "Let me give you a little piece of advice," Dwight Christian said when Paul Christian took up Dick Ziegler's side in this matter. " 'Life can only be understood backwards, but it must be lived forwards.' Kierkegaard." Dwight Christian had an actual file of such quotations, most of them torn from the "Thoughts on the Business of Life" page in *Forbes* and given to a secretary to be typed out on three-by-five index cards. The cards were his hedge against a profound shyness. "Recently I ran across a thought from Racine," he would say on those occasions when he was called upon to chair a stockholders' meeting or to keynote the Kickoff Dinner for Punahou School Annual Giving or to have his picture taken, wearing a silk suit tailored in Hong Kong and an aluminum hard hat stencilled "D.C.," knee-deep in silica sand in the hold of a dry-bulk carrier.

That particular photograph appeared in *Business Week*, at the time Dwight Christian was trying (unsuccessfully, it turned out) to take over British Leyland.

I also had two photographs from *Fortune*, one showing Dwight Christian riding a crane over a cane field and the other showing him astride an eighteen-thousand-ton concrete dolos, with a Pan American Cargo Clipper overhead.

In fact I had a number of photographs of the Christians: in that prosperous and self-absorbed colony the Christians were sufficiently good-looking and sufficiently confident and, at least at the time Inez was growing up, sufficiently innocent not to mind getting their pictures in the paper. I had Cissy Christian smoking a cigarette in a white jade holder as she presented the Christian Prize in Sugar Chemistry at the University of Hawaii in 1938. I had Dwight and Ruthie Christian tea-dancing at the Alexander Young Hotel in 1940. I had Carol Christian second-from-the-left in a group of young Honolulu matrons who met every Tuesday in 1942 to drink daiquiris and eat chicken salad and roll bandages for the Red Cross. In this photograph Carol Christian is wearing a Red Cross uniform, but in fact she was invited to join this group only twice, both times by Ruthie Christian. "Spend time around that crowd and you see how the green comes out," she said when it became clear that she would not be included on a regular basis. "You see how the green comes out" was something Carol Christian said often. She said it whenever she divined a note of rejection or criticism or even suspended judgment in someone's response to her, or, by extension, to Inez or Janet. She seemed to believe herself the object of considerable "envy," a word Inez tried to avoid in later life, and perhaps she was.

"I detect just the slightest tinge of lime."

"Positively chartreuse."

"You find out fast enough who your friends are."

In fact it would have been hard to say who Carol Christian's friends were, since she had no friends at all who were not primarily Paul Christian's friends or Cissy Christian's friends or Dwight and Ruthie Christian's friends. "Seems like a nice enough gal," one of Paul Christian's cousins said about her when she had lived in Honolulu for ten years. "Of course I haven't known her that long."

I had, curiously, only two photographs of Paul Christian, and neither suggested the apparent confidence and innocence with which his mother and his brother and even his wife met the camera. The first showed Paul Christian playing backgammon with John Huston in Cuernavaca in 1948. Paul Christian was barefoot and dark from the sun in this snapshot, which would have been taken at roughly the time arrangements were being made for his wife to leave Honolulu on the reconditioned *Lurline*. The second photograph was taken as Paul Christian left the Honolulu YMCA in handcuffs on March 25, 1975, some hours after he fired the shots that resulted in the immediate death of Wendell Omura and the eventual death of Janet Christian Ziegler. In this photograph Paul Christian was again barefoot, and had his cuffed hands raised above his head in a posture of theatrical submission, even crucifixion; a posture so arresting, so peculiarly suggestive, that the photograph was carried in newspapers in parts of the world where there could have been no interest in the Christians or in Wendell Omura or even in Harry Victor. In most parts of the United States there was of course an interest in Harry Victor. VICTOR FAMILY TOUCHED BY ISLAND TRAGEDY, the caption read in the New York *Times*.

You see the shards of the novel I am no longer writing, the island, the family, the situation. I lost patience with it. I lost nerve. Still: there is a certain hour between afternoon and evening when the sun strikes horizontally between the trees and that island and that situation are all I see. Some days at this time one aspect of the situation will seem to me to yield the point, other days another. I see Inez Christian Victor in the spring of 1975 walking on the narrow beach behind Janet's house, the last sun ahead of her, refracted in the spray off Black Point. I see Jack Lovett watching her, a man in his sixties in a custom-made seersucker suit, his tie loosened but his bearing correct, military, suggestive of disciplines practiced for the sake of discipline; a man who is now, as he watches Inez Victor steady herself on the rocks down where the water meets the sea wall, smoking one of the five cigarettes he allows himself daily. I see Inez turn and walk back toward him, the sun behind her now, the water washing the rough coral sand over her bare feet.

I see Jack Lovett waiting for her.

I have not told you much about Jack Lovett.

Most often these days I find that my notes are about Jack Lovett, about those custom-made seersucker suits he wore, about the wide range of his interests and acquaintances and of the people to whom he routinely spoke (embassy drivers, oil riggers, airline stewardesses, assistant professors of English literature traveling on Fulbright fellowships, tropical agronomists traveling under the auspices of the Rockefeller Foundation, desk clerks and ticket agents and salesmen of rice converters and coco dryers and Dutch pesticides and German pharmaceuticals) in Manila and in Jakarta and around the Malacca Strait.

About his view of information as an end in itself.

About his access to airplanes.

About the way he could put together an observation here and a conversation there and gauge when the time had come to lay hands on a 727 or a C-46.

About the way he waited for Inez.

I have been keeping notes for some time now about the way Jack Lovett waited for Inez Victor.

4

Fırst looks are widely believed instructive. The first glimpse of someone across a room, the first view of the big house on the rise, the first meeting between the protagonists: these are considered obligatory scenes, and are meant to be remembered later, recalled to a conclusive point, recalled not only by novelists but by survivors of accidents and by witnesses to murders; recalled in fact by anyone at all forced to resort to the narrative method.

I wonder.

The first time I ever saw Jack Lovett was in a *Vogue* photographer's studio on West 40th Street, where he had come to see Inez. Under different auspices and to different ends Inez Victor and I were both working for *Vogue* that year, 1960, and although she was in the fashion department and I was upstairs in the afterthought cubicle that constituted the feature department we occasionally had reason (when a playwright was to be photographed as part of a fashion layout, say, or an actress was to actually model the merchandise) to do a sitting together. I recall coming late to the studio on this particular morning and finding Inez already there, sitting at a wooden table apparently oblivious to the reflector propped against her knee, to Chubby Checker on the stereo at eighty decibels, and to the model for the sitting, a fading beauty named Kiki Watt, who was having a comb-out and trying to tell Inez about some "Stanley" they both seemed to know.

"The doorbell rings at midnight, who else," Kiki screamed through the music. "Stanley."

Inez said nothing. The table at which she sat was covered with take-out bags from the delicatessen downstairs, one of which was leaking coffee, but Inez seemed not to notice. Her attention was entirely fixed on the man who sat across the table, a stranger, considerably older than we were and notably uncomfortable in the rather louche camaraderie of the studio. I had not met Harry Victor but I doubted the man was Inez's husband. I recall thinking he could be her father.

"Somebody strike the music," Kiki screamed. "Now. You can hear me. So. I said I had this sitting at dawn, but you know Stanley, Stanley had to have a drink. Naturally."

"Naturally." Inez looked at me. "This is Jack Lovett. He just got off a plane."

Jack Lovett stood up, trying to acknowledge me without looking at Kiki, who had dropped her wrapper and was working pieces of cotton into her brassiere.

" 'This place is a pigsty,' Stanley announces halfway through his drink." Kiki sat on the table between Inez and Jack Lovett and began rummaging through the take-out bags. " 'The maid didn't come,' I say. 'I don't suppose you own a vacuum,' Stanley says, ho hum, sarcasm, so interesting. 'Actually no,' I say. 'I don't own a vacuum.' As a matter of fact I don't, I mean I did but Gus pawned it with my jewelry. 'Listen,' Stanley says. 'As soon as Daisy leaves for Maine I'll bring over our vacuum. For the summer,' he says. Believe it?"

"Absolutely," Inez said. She took a doughnut from one of the take-out bags and held it out to Jack Lovett. Jack Lovett shook his head.

"Stanley left, I thought about it, I wanted to kill myself, you know?"

"Absolutely." Inez took a bite from the doughnut, then dropped it back into the bag.

"Wanted to take every red I had in the apartment, you know why?"

"Because you didn't want to use Daisy's vacuum," Inez said, and then she looked at me. "He has two hours in New York and he came to see me."

She turned back to Jack Lovett and smiled.

I had known Inez Victor for perhaps a year but I had never before seen her smile that way.

"He can't stay," she said then. "Because he's running a little coup somewhere. I just bet."

There it is, the first look.

The instructiveness of the moment remains moot.

Actually I know a lot about Jack Lovett.

Some men (fewer women) are solitary, unattached to any particular place or institution, most comfortable not exactly alone but in the presence of strangers. They are comfortable for example on airplanes. They buckle in, establish certain ground rules with the cabin crew (to be woken or not woken, extra ice or none, a reading light that works and a move after Singapore to the bulkhead seat); stake out blankets, pillows, territory. They are solaced by the menus with the Dong Kingman water colors on the cover, by the soothing repetition of the meal (*Rôti au Vol, Legumes Garnis*) at arbitrary intervals during flights that run eleven, twelve, twenty-two hours. A flight of fewer than eight hours is a hop, a trip these men barely recognize. On the ground they seem easy only in hotel lobbies and transit lounges, in the Express Check-Ins and Clipper Clubs of the world, sealed environments in which they always remember the names of the attendants who make the drinks and arrange the connecting flights. Such men also recognize one another, and exchange desultory recollections of other travels, absent travelers.

"That joint venture in Dakar," one hears them say.

"Frank was in Dakar."

"I saw Frank in Hong Kong Friday, he'd come down out of China."

"Frank and I were in a meeting in Surabaya with this gentleman who didn't speak a word of English. He sat through this meeting nodding and smiling, you know, a regular buddha, and then he spoke the only English words I ever heard him speak. 'Six hundred million sterling,' he said."

"They all speak sterling."

"Frank takes it in stride, a real player, looks at his watch and stands up. 'You decide you want to talk a reasonable number,' Frank says to the buddha, in English you understand, 'you can reach me tonight at the Hilton.' No change of expression from the buddha. The buddha thinks Frank's going to sweat out this call in Jakarta. 'In Manila,' Frank says then. 'The Hilton in Manila.' "

They recall other Franks, other meetings, Hiltons around the world. They are reserved, wary, only professionally affable. Their responses seem pragmatic but are often peculiarly abstract, based on systems they alone understand. They view other people as wild cards, useful in the hand but dangerous in the deck, and they gravitate to occupations in which they can deal their own hand, play their own system, their own information. All information is seen as useful. Inaccurate information is in itself accurate information about the informant.

I said that Jack Lovett was one of those men for whom information was an end in itself.

He was also a man for whom the accidental did not figure.

Many people are intolerant of the accidental, but this was something more: Jack Lovett did not believe that accidents happen. In Jack Lovett's system all behavior was purposeful, and the purpose could be divined by whoever attracted the best information and read it most correctly. A Laotian village indicated on one map and omitted on another suggested not a reconnaissance oversight but a population annihilated, *x* number of men, women, and children lined up one morning between the maps and bulldozed into a common ditch. A shipment of laser mirrors from Long Beach to a firm in Hong Kong that did no laser work suggested not a wrong invoice but transshipment, re-export, the diversion of technology to unfriendly actors. All nations, to Jack Lovett, were "actors," specifically "state actors" ("non-state actors" were the real wild cards here, but in Jack Lovett's extensive experience the average non-state actor was less interested in laser mirrors than in M-16s, AK-47s, FN-FALs, the everyday implements of short-view power, and when the inductive leap to the long view was made it would probably be straight to weapons-grade uranium), and he viewed such actors abstractly, as friendly or unfriendly, committed or uncommitted; as assemblies of armaments on a large board. Asia was ten thousand tanks here, three hundred Phantoms there. The heart of Africa was an enrichment facility.

5

THE woman to whom Jack Lovett was married from 1945 until 1952 described his occupation, whenever during the course of their marriage she applied for a charge account or filled out the forms for a new gynecologist or telephone or gas connection, as "army officer." In fact Carla Lovett made a convincing army wife, a druggist's daughter from San Jose who was comfortable shopping at the commissary and spending large parts of her day at the officers' club swimming pool, indifferent to her surroundings, passive in bad climates. Fort Hood and Georgetown and Manila and Schofield Barracks were the same to Carla Lovett, particularly after a drink or two.

The woman to whom Jack Lovett was married from 1962 until 1964 was a Honolulu divorcee named Betty Bennett, a woman who lived only a few doors from Janet and Dick Ziegler on Kahala beach and with whom Janet Ziegler occasionally played bridge and discussed shopping trips to the mainland. Betty Bennett had received the Kahala house as part of the settlement from her first husband, and continued to live in it during and after her marriage to Jack Lovett, an eighteen-month crossed connection that left little impression on either of them. When Betty Bennett filed for her divorce from Jack Lovett (I say "her" divorce reflexively, I suppose because Betty Bennett was a woman who applied the possessive pronoun reflexively, as in "my house," "my 450-SL," "my wedding lunch") she described his occupation as "aircraft executive." According to Jack Lovett's visa applications in 1975 he was a businessman. According to Jack Lovett's business cards in 1975 he was a consultant in international development.

According to Jack Lovett himself he was someone who had "various irons in the fire."

Someone who kept "the usual balls in the air."

Someone who did "a little business here and there."

Someone who did what he could.

Anyone who did any reporting at all during the middle and late sixties and early seventies was apt to have run into Jack Lovett. He was a good contact. He knew a lot of things. After I finished my first novel and left *Vogue* and started reporting I actually ran into him quite a bit, most often in Honolulu but occasionally in one or another transit lounge or American embassy, and perhaps because he identified me as a friend of Inez Victor's he seemed to exempt me from his instinctive distrust of reporters. I am not saying that he ever told me anything he did not want me to know. I am saying only that we talked, and once in a while we even talked about Inez Victor. I recall one such conversation in 1971 in Honolulu and another in 1973, on a Garuda 727 that had jammed its landing gear and was in the process of dumping its fuel over the South China Sea. Jack Lovett told me for example that he considered Inez "one of the most noble" women he had ever met. I remember this specifically because the word "noble" seemed from another era, and as such surprising, and mildly amusing.

He never told me exactly what it was he did, nor would I have asked. Exactly what Jack Lovett did was tacitly understood by most people who knew him, but not discussed. Had he been listed in *Who's Who*, which he was not, even the most casual reader of his entry could have pieced together a certain pattern, discerned the traces of what intelligence people call "interest." Such an entry would have revealed odd overlapping dates, unusual posts at unusual times. There would have been the assignment to Vientiane, the missions to Haiti, Quebec, Rawalpindi. There would have been the associations with companies providing air courier service, air cargo service, aircraft parts; companies with telephone numbers that began "800" and addresses that were post-office boxes in Miami, Honolulu, Palo Alto. There would have been blank spots. The military career would have seemed erratic, off track.

Finally, such an entry would have been starred, indicating that the subject had supplied no information, for Jack Lovett supplied information only when he saw the chance, however remote, of getting information in return. When he registered at a hotel he gave as his address one or another of those post-office boxes in Miami, Honolulu, Palo Alto. The apartment he kept in Honolulu, a one-bedroom rental near Ala Moana in a building inhabited mostly by call girls, was leased in the name "Mid-Pacific Development." It was possible to see this tendency to obscure even the most inconsequential information as a professional reflex, but it was also possible to see it as something more basic, a temperamental secretiveness, a reticence that had not so much derived from Jack Lovett's occupation as led him to it. I recall a story I heard in 1973 or 1974 from a UPI photographer who had run into Jack Lovett in a Hong Kong restaurant, an upstairs place in the Wanchai district where the customers kept their bottles in a cupboard above the cash register. Jack Lovett's bottle was on his table, a quart of Johnnie Walker Black, but the name taped on the label, in his own handwriting, was "J. LOCKHART." "You don't want your name on too many bottles around town," Jack Lovett reportedly said when the photographer mentioned the tape on the label. This was a man who for more than twenty years had maintained a grave attraction to a woman whose every move was photographed.

In this context I always see Inez Victor as she looked on a piece of WNBC film showing a party on the St. Regis Roof given by the governor of New

York; some kind of afternoon party, a wedding or a christening or an anniversary, nominally private but heavily covered by the press. On this piece of film, which was made and first shown on March 18, 1975, one week exactly before Paul Christian fired the shots that set this series of events in motion, Inez Victor can be seen dancing with Harry Victor. She is wearing a navy-blue silk dress and a shiny dark straw hat with red cherries. "Marvelous," she is heard to say repeatedly on the clip.

"Marvelous day."

"You look marvelous."

"Marvelous to be here."

"Clear space for the senator," a young man in a dark suit and a rep tie keeps saying. There are several such young men in the background, all carrying clipboards. This one seems only marginally aware of Inez Victor, and his clipboard collides a number of times with her quilted shoulder bag. "Senator Victor is here as the governor's guest, give him some room *please*."

"—Taking a more active role," a young woman with a microphone repeats.

"—Senator here as the governor's guest, *please* no interviews, that's all, that's it, hold it."

The band segues into "Isn't It Romantic."

"Hold two elevators," another of the young men says.

"I'm just a private citizen," Harry Victor says.

"Marvelous," Inez Victor says.

I first saw this clip not when it was first shown but some months later, at the time Jack Lovett was in the news, when, for the two or three days it took the story of their connection to develop and play out, Inez Victor could be seen dancing on the St. Regis Roof perhaps half a dozen times between five P.M. and midnight.

6

L ET me establish Inez Victor.

Born, as you know, Inez Christian in the Territory of Hawaii on the first day of January, 1935.

Known locally as Dwight Christian's niece.

Cissy Christian's granddaughter.

Paul Christian's daughter, of course, but Paul Christian was usually in Cuernavaca or Tangier or sailing a 12.9-meter Trintella-class ketch through the Marquesas and did not get mentioned as often as his mother and his brother. Carol Christian's daughter as well, but Carol Christian had materialized from the mainland and vanished back to the mainland, a kind of famous story in that part of the world, a novel in her own right, but not the one I have in mind.

Harry Victor's wife.

Oh shit, Inez, Jack Lovett said.

Harry Victor's wife.

He said it on the late March evening in 1975 when he and Inez sat in an empty off-limits bar across the bridge from Schofield Barracks and watched the evacuation on television of one or another capital in Southeast Asia. Conflicting reports, the anchorman said. Rapidly deteriorating situation. Scenes of panic and confusion. Down the tubes, the bartender said. Bye-bye Da Nang. On the screen above the bar the helicopter lifted again and again off the roof of the American mission and Jack Lovett watched without speaking and after a while he asked the bartender to turn off the sound and plug in the jukebox. No dancing, the bartender said. I'm already off fucking limits. You're not off limits from dancing, Jack Lovett said. You're off from fencing Sansui amps to an undercover. The bartender turned down the sound and plugged in the jukebox. Jack Lovett said nothing to Inez, only looked at her for a long time and then stood up and took her hand.

The Mamas and the Papas sang "Dream a Little Dream of Me."

The helicopter lifted again off the roof of the American mission.

In this bar across the bridge from Schofield Barracks Inez did not say "marvelous" as she danced. She did not say "marvelous day" as she danced. She did not say "you look marvelous," or "marvelous to be here." She did not say anything at all as she danced, did not even dance as you or I or the agency that regulated dancing in bars might have defined dancing. She only stood with her back against the jukebox and her arms around Jack Lovett. Her hair was loose and tangled from the drive out to Schofield and the graying streak at her left temple, the streak she usually brushed under, was exposed. Her eyes were closed against the flicker from the television screen.

"Fucking Arvin finally shooting each other," the bartender said.

"Oh shit, Inez," Jack Lovett said. "Harry Victor's wife."

7

Bʏ the spring of 1975 Inez Victor had in fact been Harry Victor's wife for twenty years.

Through Harry Victor's two years with the Justice Department, through the appearance in *The New York Times Magazine* of "Justice for Whom?—A Young Lawyer Wants Out," by Harry Victor and R.W. Dillon.

Through the Neighborhood Legal Coalition that Harry Victor and Billy Dillon organized out of the storefront in East Harlem. Through the publication of *The View from the Street: Root Causes, Radical Solutions and a Modest Proposal*, by Harry Victor, Based on Studies Conducted by Harry Victor with R.W. Dillon.

Through the marches in Mississippi and in the San Joaquin Valley, through Harry Victor's successful campaigns for Congress in 1964 and 1966 and 1968, through the sit-ins at Harvard and at the Pentagon and at Dow Chemical plants in Michigan and Pennsylvania and West Virginia.

Through Harry Victor's appointment in 1969 to fill out the last three years of a Senate term left vacant by the death of the incumbent.

Through Connie Willis and through Frances Landau ("Inez, I'm asking you nice, behave, girls like that come with the life," Billy Dillon said to Inez about Connie Willis and Frances Landau), through the major fundraising in California ("Inez, I'm asking you nice, put on your tap shoes, it's big green on the barrelhead," Billy Dillon said to Inez about California), through the speaking tours and the ad hoc committees and the fact-finding missions to Jakarta and Santiago and Managua and Phnom Penh; through the failed bid for a presidential nomination in 1972 and through the mistimed angling for a good embassy (this was one occasion when Jakarta and Santiago and Managua and Phnom Penh did not spring to Harry Victor's lips) that occurred in the wreckage of that campaign.

Through the mill.

Through the wars.

Through the final run to daylight: through the maneuvering of all the above elements into a safe place on the field, into a score, into that amorphous but inspired convergence of rhetoric and celebrity known as the Alliance for Democratic Institutions.

Inez Victor had been there.

Because Inez Victor had been there many people believed that they knew her: not "most" people, since the demographics of Harry Victor's phantom constituency were based on comfort and its concomitant uneasiness, but most people of a type, most people who read certain newspapers and bought certain magazines, most people who knew what kind of girls came with the life, most people who knew where there was big green on the barrelhead, most people who were apt to have noticed Inez buying printed sheets on sale in Bloomingdale's basement or picking up stemmed strawberries at Gristede's or waiting for one of her and Harry Victor's twin children, the girl Jessie or the boy Adlai, in front of the Dalton School.

These were people who all knew exactly what Inez Victor did with the stemmed strawberries she picked up at Gristede's (passed them in a silver bowl at her famous New Year's Eve parties on Central Park West, according to *Vogue*); what Inez Victor did with the printed sheets she bought on sale in Bloomingdale's basement (cut them into round tablecloths for her famous Fourth of July parties in Amagansett, according to *W*); and what Inez Victor had paid for the Ungaro khaki shirtwaists she wore during the 1968 convention, the 1968 Chicago convention during which Harry Victor was photographed for *Life* getting tear-gassed in Grant Park.

These were people who all knew someone who knew someone who knew that on the night in 1972 when Harry Victor conceded the California primary before the polls closed Inez Victor flew back to New York on the press plane and sang "It's All Over Now, Baby Blue" with an ABC cameraman and the photographer from *Rolling Stone*.

These people had all seen Inez, via telephoto lens, drying Jessie's fine blond hair by the swimming pool at the house in Amagansett. These people had all seen Inez, in the *Daily News*, leaving Lenox Hill Hospital with Adlai on the occasion of his first automobile accident. These people had all seen photograph after photograph of the studied clutter in the library of the apartment on Central Park West, the Canton jars packed with marking pencils, the stacks of *Le Monde* and *Foreign Affairs* and *The Harvard Business Review*, the legal pads, the several telephones, the framed snapshots of Harry Victor eating barbecue with Eleanor Roosevelt and of Harry Victor crossing a police line with Coretta King and of Harry Victor playing on the beach at Amagansett with Jessie and with Adlai and with Frances Landau's Russian wolfhound.

These people had taken their toll.

By which I mean to suggest that Inez Victor had come to view most occasions as photo opportunities.

By which I mean to suggest that Inez Victor had developed certain mannerisms peculiar to people in the public eye: a way of fixing her gaze in the middle distance, a habit of smoothing her face in repose by pressing up on her temples with her middle fingers; a noticeably frequent blink, as if the photographers' strobes had triggered a continuing flash on her retina.

By which I mean to suggest that Inez Victor had lost certain details.

I recall being present one morning in a suite in the Hotel Doral in Miami, amid the debris of Harry Victor's 1972 campaign for the nomination, when a feature writer from the Associated Press asked Inez what she believed to be the "major cost" of public life.

"Memory, mainly," Inez said.

"Memory," the woman from the Associated Press repeated.

"Memory, yes. Is what I would call the major cost. Definitely." The suite in the Doral that morning was a set being struck. On a sofa that two workmen were pushing back against a wall Billy Dillon was trying to talk on the telephone. In the foyer a sound man from one of the networks was packing up equipment left the night before. "I believe I can speak for Inez when I say that we're looking forward to a period of being just plain Mr. and Mrs. Victor," Harry had said the night before on all three networks. Inez stood up now and began looking for a clean ashtray on a room-service table covered with half-filled glasses. "Something like shock treatment," she added.

"You mean you've had shock treatment."

"No. I mean you lose track. *As if* you'd had shock treatment."

"I see. 'Lose track' of what exactly?"

"Of what happened."

"I see."

"Of what you said. And didn't say."

"I see. Yes. During the campaign."

"Well, no. During your—" Inez looked at me for help. I pretended to be absorbed in the Miami *Herald*. Inez emptied a dirty ashtray into the lid of a film can and sat down again. "During your whole life."

"You mentioned shock treatment. You haven't personally—"

"I said no. Didn't I say no? I said 'as if.' I said

'something like.' I meant you drop fuel. You jettison cargo. Eject the crew. You *lose track*."

There was a silence. Billy Dillon cradled the telephone against his shoulder and mimed a backhand volley. "It's a game, Inez, it's tennis," Billy Dillon always said to Inez about interviews. It was a routine between them. I had seen him do it that morning, when Inez said that since I had come especially to see her she did not want to do the AP interview. "Sure you do," Billy Dillon had said. "It's only going to last x minutes. Finite time. For those x minutes you're here to play. You're going to place the ball"—here Billy Dillon had paused, and executed a shadow serve—"inside the lines. The major cost of public life is privacy, Inez, that's an easy shot. The hardest part about Washington life is finding a sitter for the Gridiron Dinner. The fun part about Washington life is taking friends from home to the Senate cafeteria for navy-bean soup. You've tried the recipe at home but it never tastes the same. Yes, you do collect recipes. Yes, you do worry about the rising cost of feeding a family. Ninety-nine per cent of the people you know in Washington are basically concerned with the rising cost of feeding a family. Schools. Mortgages. Programs. You've always viewed victory as a mandate not for a man but for his programs. Now: you view defeat with mixed emotions. Why: because you've learned to treasure the private moments."

"*Private moments*," Billy Dillon mouthed silently in the suite at the Hotel Doral.

Inez looked deliberately away from Billy Dillon.

"Here's an example." She lit a match, watched it burn, and blew it out. "You looked up the clips on me before you came here."

"I did a little homework, yes." The woman's finger hovered over the stop button on her tape recorder. Now it was she who looked to me for help. I looked out the window. "Naturally. That's my business. We all do."

"That's my point."

"I'm afraid I don't quite—"

"Things that might or might not be true get repeated in the clips until you can't tell the difference."

"But that's why I'm here. I'm not writing a piece from the clips. I'm writing a piece based on what you tell me."

"You might as well write it from the clips," Inez said. Her voice was reasonable. "Because I've lost track. Which is what I said in the first place."

INEZ VICTOR CLAIMS SHE IS OFTEN MISQUOTED, is the way that went out on the Associated Press wire. "Somebody up there likes you, it doesn't say INEZ VICTOR DENIES SHOCK TREATMENT," Billy Dillon said when he read it.

8

I HAVE never been sure what Inez thought about how her days were passed during those years she spent in Washington and New York. The idea of "expressing" herself seems not to have occurred to her. She held the occasional job but pursued no particular work. Even the details of running a household did not engage her unduly. Her houses were professionally kept and, for all the framed snapshots and studied clutter, entirely impersonal, expressive not of some individual style but only of the conventions then current among the people she saw. Nothing of the remote world in which she had grown up intruded on the world in which she later found herself: the Christians, like many island families, had surrounded themselves with the mementos of their accomplishments, with water colors and painted tea cups and evidence of languages mastered and instruments played, framed recital programs and letters of commendation and the souvenirs of wedding trips and horse shows and trips to China, and it was the absence of any such jetsam that was eccentric in Inez's houses, as if she had buckled her seat belt and the island had dematerialized beneath her.

Of course there were rumors about her. She liked

painters, and usually had a table or two of them at her big parties, and a predictable number of people said that she had had an affair with this one or that one or all of them. According to Inez she never had. I know for a fact that she never had what was called a "problem about drinking," another rumor, but the story that she did persisted, partly because Harry Victor did so little to discourage it. At a crowded restaurant in the East Fifties for example Harry Victor was heard asking Inez if she intended to drink her dinner. In that piece of WNBC film shot on the St. Regis Roof, another example, Harry Victor is seen taking a glass of champagne from Inez's hand and passing it out of camera range.

Inez remained indifferent. She seemed to dwell as little on the rest of her life as she did on her jobs, which she tried and abandoned like seasonal clothes. When Harry Victor was in the Justice Department Inez worked, until the twins were born, in a docent capacity at the National Gallery. When Harry Victor left the Justice Department and came up to New York Inez turned up at *Vogue*, and was given one of those jobs that fashion magazines then kept for well-connected young women in unsettled circumstances, women who needed a place to pass the time between houses or marriages or lunches. Later she did a year at Parke-Bernet. She served on the usual boards, benefit committees, commissions for the preservation of wilderness and the enhancement of opportunity; when it became clear that Harry Victor would be making the run for the nomination and that Inez would need what

Billy Dillon called a special interest, she insisted, un-expectedly and with considerable vehemence, that she wanted to work with refugees, but it was decided that refugees were an often controversial and therefore in-appropriate special interest.

Instead, because Inez was conventionally interested in and by that time moderately knowledgeable about painting, she was named a consultant for the collec-tion of paintings that hung in American embassies and residences around the world. In theory the wives of new ambassadors would bring Inez the measurements, furnished by the State Department, of the walls they needed to fill, and Inez would offer advice on which paintings best suited not only the wall space but the mood of the post. "Well, for example, I wouldn't nec-essarily think of sending a Sargent to Zaire," she ex-plained to an interviewer, but she was hard put to say why. In any case only two new ambassadors were named during Inez's tenure as consultant, which made this special interest less than entirely absorbing. As for wanting to work with refugees, she finally did, in Kuala Lumpur, and it occurred to me when I saw her there that Inez Victor had herself been a kind of refugee. She had the protective instincts of a success-ful refugee. She never looked back.

9

OR at least almost never.

I know of one occasion on which Inez Victor did in fact try to look back.

A try, an actual effort.

This effort was, for Inez, uncharacteristically systematic, and took place on the redwood deck of the borrowed house in which Harry and Inez Victor stayed the spring he lectured at Berkeley, between the 1972 campaign and the final funding of the Alliance for Democratic Institutions. It had begun with a quarrel after a faculty dinner in Harry's honor. "I've always tried to talk up to the American people," Harry had said when a physicist at the table questioned his approach to one or another energy program, and it had seemed to Inez that a dispirited pall fell over what had been, given the circumstances, a lively and pleasant evening.

"Not down," Harry had added. "You talk down to the American people at your peril."

The physicist had pressed his point, which was technical, and abstruse.

"Either Jefferson was right or he wasn't," Harry had said. "I happen to believe he was."

In fact Inez had heard Harry say this a number of

times before, usually when he had no facts at hand, and she might never have remarked on it had Harry not mentioned the physicist on the drive home.

"Hadn't done his homework," Harry had said. "Those guys get their Nobels and start coasting."

Inez, who was driving, said nothing.

"Unless there's something behind us I don't know about," Harry said as she turned into San Luis Road, "you might try lightening up the foot on the gas pedal."

"Unless you're running for something I don't know about," Inez heard herself say, "you might try lightening up the rhetoric at the dinner table."

There had been a silence.

"That wasn't necessary," Harry said finally, his voice at first stiff and hurt, and then, marshalling for second strike: "I don't really care if you take out your quite palpable unhappiness on me, but I'm glad the children are in New York."

"Away from my quite palpable unhappiness I suppose you mean."

"On the money."

They had gone to bed in silence, and, the next morning, after Harry left for the campus without speaking, Inez took her coffee and a package of cigarettes out into the sun on the redwood deck and sat down to consider the phrase "quite palpable unhappiness." It did not seem to her that she was palpably unhappy, but neither did it seem that she was palpably happy. "Happiness" and "unhappiness" did not even seem to be cards in the hand she normally played, and there on the deck in the thin morning sunlight she resolved to reconstruct the details of occasions on which she recalled being happy. As she considered such occasions she was struck by their insignificance, their absence of application to the main events of her life. In retrospect she seemed to have been most happy in borrowed houses, and at lunch.

She recalled being extremely happy eating lunch by herself in a hotel room in Chicago, once when snow was drifting on the window ledges. There was a lunch in Paris that she remembered in detail: a late lunch with Harry and the twins at Pré Catelan in the rain. She remembered rain streaming down the big windows, rain blowing in the trees, the branches brushing the glass and the warm light inside. She remembered Jessie crowing with delight and pointing imperiously at a poodle seated on a gilt chair across the room. She remembered Harry unbuttoning Adlai's wet sweater, kissing Jessie's wet hair, pouring them each a half glass of white wine.

There was an entire day in Hong Kong that she managed to reconstruct, a day she had spent alone with Jessie in a borrowed house overlooking Repulse Bay. She and Harry had dropped Adlai in Honolulu with Janet and Dick Ziegler and they had bundled Jessie onto a plane to Hong Kong and when they landed at dawn they learned that Harry was expected in Saigon for a situation briefing. Harry had flown immediately down to Saigon and Inez had waited with Jessie in this house that belonged to the chief of the *Time* bureau in Hong Kong. The potted begonias outside that house had made Inez happy and the parched lawn made her happy and the particular cast of the sun on the sea made her happy and it even made her happy that the *Time* bureau chief had mentioned, as he gave her the keys at the airport, that baby cobras had recently been seen in the garden. This introduction of baby cobras into the day had lent Inez a sense of transcendent usefulness, a reason to carry Jessie wherever Jessie wanted to go. She had carried Jessie from the porch to the swing in the garden. She had carried Jessie from the swing in the garden to the bench from which they could watch the sun on the sea. She had carried Jessie even from the house to the government car that returned at sundown to take them to the hotel where Harry was due at midnight.

There in the sun on the redwood deck on San Luis Road Inez began to think of Berkeley as another place in which she might later remember being extremely happy, another borrowed house, and she resolved to keep this in mind, but by June of that year, back in New York, she was already losing the details. That was the June during which Adlai had the accident (the second accident, the bad one, the accident in which the fifteen-year-old from Denver lost her left eye and the function of one kidney), and it was also the June, 1973, during which Inez found Jessie on the floor of her bedroom with the disposable needle and the glassine envelope in her Snoopy wastebasket.

"Let me die and get it over with," Jessie said. "Let me be in the ground and go to sleep."

The doctor came in a sweat suit.

"I got a D in history," Jessie said. "Nobody sits with me at lunch. Don't tell Daddy."

"I'm right here," Harry said.

"Daddy's right here," Inez said.

"Don't tell Daddy," Jessie said.

"It might be useful to talk about therapy," the doctor said.

"It might also be useful to assign some narcs to the Dalton School," Harry said. "No. Strike that. Don't quote me."

"This is a stressful time," the doctor said.

The first therapist the doctor recommended was a young woman attached to a clinic on East 61st Street that specialized in the treatment of what the therapist called adolescent substance abuse. "It might be useful to talk about you," the therapist said. "Your own life, how you perceive it."

Inez remembered that the therapist was wearing a silver ankh.

She remembered that she could see Jessie through a glass partition, chewing on a strand of her long blond hair, bent over the Minnesota Multiphasic Personality Inventory.

"My life isn't really the problem at hand," she remembered saying. "Is it?"

The therapist smiled.

Inez lit a cigarette.

It occurred to her that if she just walked into the next room and took Jessie by the hand and got her on a plane somewhere, still wearing her Dalton School sweat shirt, the whole thing might blow over. They could go meet Adlai in Colorado Springs. Adlai had gone back to Colorado Springs the day before, for summer session at the school where he was trying to accumulate enough units to get into a college accredited for draft deferment. They could go meet Harry in Ann Arbor. Harry had left for Ann Arbor that morning, to deliver his lecture on the uses and misuses of civil disobedience. "I can't get through to her," Harry had said before he left for Ann Arbor. "Adlai may be a fuck-up, but I can talk to Adlai. I talk to her, I'm talking to a UFO."

"Adlai," Inez had said, "happens to believe that he can satisfy his American History requirement with a three-unit course called History of American Film."

"Very good, Inez. Broad, but good."

"Broad, but true. In addition to which. Moreover. I asked Adlai to make a point of going to the hospital to see Cynthia. Here's what he said."

"Cynthia who?" Harry said.

"Cynthia who he almost killed in the accident. 'She's definitely on the agenda.' Is what he said."

"At least he said something. All you'd get from her is the stare."

"You always say *her*. Her name is Jessie."

"*I know her goddamn name.*"

Strike Ann Arbor.

Harry would be sitting around in his shirtsleeves expressing admiration ("Admiration, Christ no, what I feel when I see you guys is a kind of *awe*") for the most socially responsible generation ever to hit American campuses.

Strike Colorado Springs.

Adlai already had his agenda.

Jessie looked up from the Minnesota Multiphasic Personality Inventory and smiled fleetingly at the glass partition.

"The 'problem at hand,' as you put it, is substance habituation." The therapist opened a drawer and extracted an ashtray and slid it across the desk toward Inez. She was still smiling. "I notice you smoke."

"I do, yes." Inez crushed out the cigarette and stood up. Jessie's complexion was clear and her hair was like honey and there was no way of telling that beneath the sleeves of the Dalton School sweatshirt there were needle tracks visible on her smooth tanned arms. "I also drink coffee."

The therapist's expression did not change.

Let me die and get it over with.

Let me be in the ground and go to sleep.

Don't tell Daddy.

Inez picked up her jacket.

On the other side of the glass partition Jessie took a pocket mirror from her shoulder bag and began lining her eyes with the IBM testing pencil.

"What I don't do is shoot heroin," Inez said.

The second therapist believed that the answer lay in a closer examination of the sibling gestalt. The third employed a technique incorporating elements of aversion therapy. At the clinic in Seattle to which Jessie was finally sent in the fall of 1974, a private facility specializing in the treatment of what the fourth therapist called adolescent chemical dependency, the staff referred to the patients as clients, maintained them on methadone, and obtained for them part-time jobs "suited to the character structure and particular skills of the individual client." Jessie's job was as a waitress in a place on Puget Sound called King Crab's Castle. "Pretty cinchy," Jessie said on the telephone, "if you can keep the pickled beet slice from running into the crab louis."

The bright effort in Jessie's voice had constricted Inez's throat.

"It's all experience," Inez said finally, and Jessie giggled.

"Really," Jessie said, emphasizing the word to suggest agreement. She was not yet eighteen.

10

O T H E R costs.

Inez had stopped staying alone in the apartment on Central Park West after the superintendent told a reporter from *Newsday* that he had let himself in to drain a radiator and Mrs. Victor had asked him to fix her a double vodka. She took fingernail scissors and scratched the label off empty prescription bottles before she threw them in the trash. She stopped patronizing a bookstore on Madison Avenue after she noticed the names, addresses, and delivery instructions for all the customers, including herself ("doorman— Lloyd, maid lvs at 4") in an open account book by the cash register. She would not allow letters that came unsolicited from strangers to be opened inside the apartment, or packages that came from anyone. She had spoken to Billy Dillon about the possibility of suing *People* for including Adlai's accidents in an article on the problems of celebrity children, and also of enjoining *Who's Who* to delete mention of herself and Jessie and Adlai from Harry Victor's entry. "I don't quite see the significance, Inez," Billy Dillon had said. "Since I see your name in the paper two, three times a week minimum."

"The significance is," Inez said, "that some stranger

might be sitting in a library somewhere reading *Who's Who*."

"Consider this stranger your bread and butter, an interested citizen," Billy Dillon said, but Inez never could. Strangers remembered. Strangers suffered disappointments, and became confused. A stranger might suffer a disappointment too deep to be lanced by a talk with *Newsday*, and become confused. Life outside camera range, life as it was lived by (Inez imagined then) her father and her Uncle Dwight and her sister Janet, had become for Inez only a remote idea, something she knew about but did not entirely comprehend. She did not for example comprehend how her father could give her telephone number to strangers he met on airplanes, and then call to remonstrate with her when he heard she had been short on the telephone. "I think you might have spared ten minutes," Paul Christian had said on one such call. "This young man you hung up on happens to have a quite interesting grassy-knoll slant on Sal Mineo's murder, he very much wanted Harry to hear it." She did not for example comprehend what moved Dwight to send her a clipping of every story in the Honolulu *Advertiser* in which her or Harry's name appeared. These clippings came in bundles, with Dwight's card attached. "Nice going," he sometimes pencilled on the card. Nor did she comprehend how Janet could have agreed, during the 1972 campaign, to be interviewed on *CBS Reports* about her and Inez's childhood. This particular *CBS Reports* had been devoted to capsule biographies of the candidates' wives and Inez had watched it with Harry and Billy Dillon in the library of the apartment on Central Park West. There had been a clip of Harry talking about Inez's very special loyalty and there had been a clip of Billy Dillon talking about Inez's very special feeling for the arts and there had been a clip of the headmaster at the Dalton School talking about the very special interest Inez took in education, but Janet's appearance on the program was a surprise.

"I wouldn't say 'privileged,' no," Janet had said on camera. She had seemed to be sitting barefoot on a catamaran in front of her beach house. "No. Off the mark. Not 'privileged.' I'd just call it a marvelous simple way of life that you might describe as gone with the wind."

"I hope nobody twigs she's talking about World War Two," Billy Dillon said.

"Of course everybody had their marvelous Chinese amah then," Janet was saying on camera. Her voice was high and breathy and nervous. The camera angle had changed to show Koko Head. Inez picked up a legal pad and began writing. "And then Nezzie and I had—oh, I suppose a sort of governess, a French governess, she was from Neuilly, needless to say Mademoiselle spoke flawless French, I remember Nezzie used to drive her wild by speaking pidgin."

" 'Mademoiselle,' " Billy Dillon said.

Inez did not look up from the legal pad.

" 'Mademoiselle,' " Billy Dillon repeated, "and 'Nezzie.' "

"I was never called 'Nezzie.' "

"You are now," Billy Dillon said.

"They pan left," Harry Victor said, "they could pick up Janet's private-property-no-trespassing-no-beach-access sign." He reached under the table to pick up the telephone. "Also her Mercedes. This should be Mort."

"Ask Mort how he thinks the governess from Neuilly tests out," Billy Dillon said. "Possibly Janet could make Mademoiselle available to do some coffees in West Virginia."

Inez said nothing.

She had never been called Nezzie.

She had never spoken pidgin.

The governess from Neuilly had not been a governess at all but the French wife of a transport pilot at Hickam who rented the studio over Cissy Christian's garage for a period of six months between the Leyte Gulf and the end of the war.

Janet was telling *CBS Reports* how she and Inez had been taught to store table linens between sheets of blue tissue paper.

Harry was on his evening conference call with Mort Goldman at MIT and Perry Young at Harvard and the petrochemical people at Stanford.

No Nezzie.

No pidgin.

No governess from Neuilly.

"That tip about the blue tissue paper goes straight to the hearts and minds," Billy Dillon said.

"Mort still sees solar as negative policy, Billy, maybe you better pick up," Harry Victor said.

"Tell Mort we just kiss it," Billy Dillon said. "Broad strokes only. Selected venues." He watched as Inez tore the top sheet from the legal pad on which she had been writing. "Strictly for the blue-tissue-paper crowd."

1) Shining Star, Inez had written on the piece of paper.

2) Twinkling Star

3) Morning Star

4) Evening Star

5) Southern Star

6) North Star

7) Celestial Star

8) Meridian Star

9) Day Star

10) ? ? ?

"Hey," Billy Dillon said. "Inez. If you're drafting a cable to Janet, tell her we're retiring her number."

"Mort's raising a subtle point here, Billy," Harry Victor said. "Pick up a phone."

Inez crumpled the piece of paper and threw it into the fire. On the day Carol Christian left for good on the *Lurline* Janet had not stopped crying until she was taken from the Pacific Club to the pediatrician's office and sedated, but Inez never did cry. *Aloha oe.* I am talking here about a woman who believed that grace would descend on those she loved and peace upon her household on the day she remembered the names of all ten Star Ferry boats that crossed between Hong Kong and Kowloon. She could never get the tenth. The tenth should have been *Night Star*, but was not.

During the 1972 campaign and even later I thought of Inez Victor's capacity for passive detachment as an affectation born of boredom, the frivolous habit of an essentially idle mind. After the events which occurred in the spring and summer of 1975 I thought of it differently. I thought of it as the essential mechanism for living a life in which the major cost was memory. Drop fuel. Jettison cargo. Eject crew.

11

I N the spring of 1975, during the closing days of what Jack Lovett called "the assistance effort" in Vietnam, I happened to be teaching at Berkeley, lecturing on the same short-term basis on which Harry Victor had lectured there between the 1972 campaign and the final funding of the Alliance for Democratic Institutions; living alone in a room at the Faculty Club and meeting a dozen or so students in the English Department to discuss the idea of democracy in the work of certain post-industrial writers. I spent my classroom time pointing out similarities in style, and presumably in ideas of democracy (the hypothesis being that the way a writer constructed a sentence reflected the way that writer thought), between George Orwell and Ernest Hemingway, Henry Adams and Norman Mailer. "The hills opposite us were grey and wrinkled like the skins of elephants" and "this war was a racket like all other wars" were both George Orwell, but were also an echo of Ernest Hemingway. "Probably no child, born in the year, held better cards than he" and "he began to feel the forty-foot dynamo as a moral force, much as the early Christians felt the Cross" were both Henry Adams, but struck a note that would reverberate in Norman Mailer.

What did this tell us, I asked my class.

Consider the role of the writer in a post-industrial society.

Consider the political implications of both the reliance on and the distrust of abstract words, consider the social organization implicit in the use of the autobiographical third person.

Consider, too, Didion's own involvement in the setting: an atmosphere results. How? It so happened that I had been an undergraduate at Berkeley, which meant that twenty years before in the same room or one like it (high transoms and golden oak moldings and cigarette scars on the floor, sixty years of undergraduate yearnings not excluding my own) I had considered the same questions or ones like them. In 1955 on this campus I had first noticed the quickening of time. In 1975 time was no longer just quickening but collapsing, falling in on itself, the way a disintegrating star contracts into a black hole, and at the scene of all I had left unlearned I could summon up only fragments of poems, misremembered. Apologies to A.E. Housman, T.S. Eliot, Delmore Schwartz:

> Of my three-score years and ten
> These twenty would not come again.
> Black wing, brown wing, hover over
> Twenty years and the spring is over.
> This was the school in which we learned
> That time was the fire in which we burned.

Sentimental sojourn.

Less time left for those visions and revisions.

In this rather febrile mood I seemed able to concentrate only on reading newspapers, specifically on reading the dispatches from Southeast Asia, finding in those falling capitals a graphic instance of the black hole effect. I said "falling." Many of the students to whom I spoke said "being liberated." "The establishment press has been giving us some joyous news," one said, and when next we spoke I modified "falling" to "closing down."

Every morning I walked from the Faculty Club to a newsstand off Telegraph Avenue to get the San Francisco *Chronicle*, the Los Angeles *Times*, and the New York *Times*. Every afternoon I got the same dispatches, under new headlines and with updated leads, in the San Francisco *Examiner*, the Oakland *Tribune*, and the Berkeley *Gazette*. Tank battalions vanished between editions. Three hundred fixed-wing aircraft disappeared in the new lead on a story about the president playing golf at the El Dorado Country Club in Palm Desert, California.

I would skim the stories on policy and fix instead on details: the cost of a visa to leave Cambodia in the weeks before Phnom Penh closed was five hundred dollars American. The colors of the landing lights for the helicopters on the roof of the American embassy in Saigon were red, white, and blue. The code names for the American evacuations of Cambodia and Vietnam respectively were EAGLE PULL and FREQUENT WIND. The amount of cash burned in the courtyard of the DAO in Saigon before the last helicopter left was three-and-a-half million dollars American and eighty-five million piastres. The code name for this operation was MONEY BURN. The number of Vietnamese soldiers who managed to get aboard the last American 727 to leave Da Nang was three hundred and thirty. The number of Vietnamese soldiers to drop from the wheel wells of the 727 was one. The 727 was operated by World Airways. The name of the pilot was Ken Healy.

I read such reports over and over again, pinned in the repetitions and dislocations of the breaking story as if in the beam of a runaway train, but I read only those stories that seemed to touch, however peripherally, on Southeast Asia. All other news receded, went unmarked and unread, and, if the first afternoon story about Paul Christian killing Wendell Omura had not been headlined CONGRESSIONAL FOE OF VIET CONFLICT SHOT IN HONOLULU, I might never have read it at all. Janet Ziegler was not mentioned that first afternoon but she was all over the morning editions and so, photographs in the *Chronicle* and a separate sidebar in the New York *Times*, VICTOR FAMILY TOUCHED BY ISLAND TRAGEDY, were Inez and Harry Victor.

That was March 26, 1975.

A Wednesday morning.

I tried to call Inez Victor in New York but Inez was already gone.

12

S ᴇ ᴇ it this way.

See the sun rise that Wednesday morning in 1975 the way Jack Lovett saw it.

From the operations room at the Honolulu airport.

The warm rain down on the runways.

The smell of jet fuel.

The military charters, Jack Lovett's excuse for being in the operations room at the airport, C-130s, DC-8s, already coming in from Saigon all night long now, clustered around the service hangars.

The first light breaking on the sea, throwing into relief two islands (first one and then, exactly ninety seconds later, the second, two discrete land masses visible on the southeastern horizon only during those two or three minutes each day when the sun rises behind them.

The regularly scheduled Pan American 747 from Kennedy via LAX banking over the milky shallows and touching down, on time, the big wheels spraying up water from the tarmac, the slight skidding, the shudder as the engines cut down.

Five-thirty-seven A.M.

The ground crew in thin yellow slickers.

The steps wheeled into place.

The passenger service representative waiting at the bottom of the steps, carrying an umbrella, a passenger manifest in a protective vinyl envelope and, over his left arm, one plumeria lei.

The woman for whom both the passenger service representative and Jack Lovett are watching (Jack Lovett's excuse for being in the operations room at the airport is not the same as Jack Lovett's reason for being in the operations room at the airport) will be the next-to-last passenger off the plane. She is a woman at that age (a few months over forty in her case) when it is possible to look very good at certain times of day (Sunday lunch in the summertime is a good time of day for such women, particularly if they wear straw hats that shade their eyes and silk shirts that cover their elbows and if they resist the inclination to another glass of white wine after lunch) and not so good at other times of day. Five-thirty-seven A.M. is not a good time of day for this woman about to de-plane the Pan American 747. She is bare-legged, pale despite one of those year-round suntans common among American women of some means, and she is wearing sling-heeled pumps, one of which has loos-ened and slipped down on her heel. Her dark hair, clearly brushed by habit to minimize the graying streak at her left temple, is dry and lustreless from the night spent on the airplane. She is wearing no makeup. She is wearing dark glasses. She is wearing a short knitted skirt and jacket, with a cotton jersey beneath the jacket, and at the moment she steps from the cabin of the plane into the moist warmth of the rainy tropical morning she takes off the jacket and leans to adjust the heel strap of her shoe. As the passenger service representative starts up the steps with the umbrella she straightens and glances back, apparently confused.

The man behind her on the steps, the man whose name appears on the manifest as DILLON, R.W., leans toward her and murmurs briefly.

She looks up, smiles at the passenger service representative, and leans forward, docile, while he attempts to simultaneously shield her with the umbrella and place the plumeria lei on her shoulders.

Aloha, he would be saying.

So kind.

Tragic circumstances.

Anything we as a company or I personally can do.

Facilitate arrangements.

When the senator arrives.

So kind.

As the passenger service representative speaks to the man listed on the manifest as DILLON, R.W., clearly a consultation about cars, baggage, facilitating arrangements, when the senator arrives, the woman stands slightly apart, still smiling dutifully. She has stepped beyond the protection of the umbrella and the rain runs down her face and hair. Absently she fingers the flowers of the lei, lifts them to her face, presses the petals against her cheek and crushes them. She will still be wearing the short knitted skirt and the crushed lei when she sees, two hours later, through a glass window in the third-floor intensive care unit at Queen's Medical Center, the unconscious body of her sister Janet.

This scene is my leper at the door, my Tropical Belt Coal Company, my lone figure on the crest of the immutable hill.

Inez Victor at 5:47 A.M. on the morning of March 26, 1975, crushing her lei in the rain on the runway.

Jack Lovett watching her.

"Get her in out of the goddamn rain," Jack Lovett said to no one in particular.

TWO

1

On the occasion when Dwight Christian
seemed to me most explicitly himself he was smoking
a long Havana cigar and gazing with evident satisfac-
tion at the steam rising off the lighted swimming pool
behind the house on Manoa Road. The rising steam
and the underwater lights combined to produce an
unearthly glow on the surface of the pool, bubbling
luridly around the filter outflow; since the air that
evening was warm the water temperature must have
been, to give off steam, over one hundred. I recall
asking Dwight Christian how (meaning why) he happened to keep the pool so hot. "No trick to heat a
pool," Dwight Christian said, as if I had congratulated
him. In fact Dwight Christian tended to interpret anything said to him by a woman as congratulation.
"Trick is to cool one down."

It had not occurred to me, I said, that a swimming
pool might need cooling down.

"Haven't spent time in the Gulf, I see." Dwight
Christian rocked on his heels. "In the Gulf you have
to cool them down, we developed the technology at
Dhahran. Pioneered it for Aramco. Cost-efficient.
Used it there and in Dubai. Had to. Otherwise we'd
have sizzled our personnel."

A certain dreaminess entered his gaze for an instant, an involuntary softening at the evocation of Dhahran, Dubai, cost-efficient technology for Aramco, and then, quite abruptly, he made a harsh guttural noise, apparently intended as the sound of sizzling personnel, and laughed.

That was Dwight Christian.

"Visited DWIGHT and Ruthie (Mills College '33) CHRISTIAN at their very gracious island outpost, he has changed the least of our classmates over the years and is still Top Pineapple on the hospitality front," as an item I saw recently in the Stanford alumni notes had it.

On the occasion when Harry Victor seemed to me most explicitly himself he was patronizing the governments of western Europe at a dinner table on Tregunter Road in London. "Sooner or later they all show up with their shopping lists," he said, over *rijstaffel* on blue willow plates and the weak Scotch and soda he was nursing through dinner. He had arrived at dinner that evening not with Inez but with a young woman he identified repeatedly as "a grandniece of the first Jew on the Supreme Court of the United States." The young woman was Frances Landau. Frances Landau listened to everything Harry Victor said with studied attention, breaking her gaze only to provide glosses for the less attentive, her slightly hyperthyroid face sharp in the candlelight and her voice intense, definite, an insistent echo of every opinion she had ever heard expressed.

"What they want, in other words," Frances Landau said. "From the United States."

"Which is usually nuclear fuel," Harry Victor said, picking up a dessert spoon and studying the marking. He seemed to find Frances Landau's rapt interpolation suddenly wearing. He was not an insensitive man but he had the obtuse confidence, the implacable ethnocentricity, of many people who have spent time in Washington. "I slept last night on a carrier in the Indian Ocean," he had said several times before dinner. The implication seemed to be that he had slept on the carrier so that London might sleep free, and I was struck by the extent to which he seemed to perceive the Indian Ocean, the carrier, and even himself as abstracts, incorporeal extensions of policy.

"Nuclear fuel to start up their breeders," he added now, and then, quite inexplicably to the other guests, he launched as if by reflex into the lines from an Auden poem that he had been incorporating that year into all his public utterances: " 'I and the public know what all schoolchildren learn. Those to whom evil is done do evil in return.' W.H. Auden. But I don't have to tell you that." He paused. "The English poet."

That was Harry Victor.

My point is this: I can remember a moment in which Harry Victor seemed to present himself precisely as he was and I can remember a moment in which Dwight Christian seemed to present himself precisely as he was and I can remember such moments about most people I have known, so ingrained by now is the impulse to define the personality, show the character, but I have no memory of any one moment in which either Inez Victor or Jack Lovett seemed to spring out, defined. They were equally evanescent, in some way emotionally invisible; unattached, wary to the point of opacity, and finally elusive. They seemed not to belong anywhere at all, except, oddly, together.

They had met in Honolulu during the winter of 1952. I can define exactly how winter comes to Honolulu: a kona wind comes up and the season changes. *Kona* means leeward, and this particular wind comes off the leeward side of the island, muddying the reef, littering the beaches with orange peels and prophylactics and bits of Styrofoam cups, knocking blossoms from the plumeria trees and dry fronds from the palms. The sea goes milky. Termites swarm on wooden roofs. The temperature has changed only slightly, but only tourists swim. At the edge of the known world there is only water, water as a definite presence, water as the end to which even the island will eventually come, and a certain restlessness prevails. Men like Dwight Christian watch the steam rise off their swimming pools and place more frequent calls to project sites in Taipei, Penang, Jedda. Women like Ruthie Christian take their furs out of storage, furs handed down from mother to daughter virtually unworn, the guard hairs still intact, and imagine trips to the mainland. It is during these days and nights when sheets of rain obscure the horizon and the surf rises on the north shore that the utter isolation of the place seems most profound, and it was on such a night, in 1952, that Jack Lovett first saw Inez Christian, and discerned in the grain of her predictable longings and adolescent vanities an eccentricity, a secretiveness, an emotional solitude to match his own. I see now.

I learned some of this from him.

January 1, 1952.

Intermission at the ballet, one of those third-string touring companies that afford the women and children and dutiful providers of small cities an annual look at "Afternoon of a Faun" and the Grand Pas de Deux from the "Nutcracker"; an occasion, a benefit, a reason to dress up after the general fretfulness of the season and the specific lassitude of the holiday and stand outside beneath an improvised canopy drinking champagne from paper cups. Subdued greetings. Attenuated attention. Cissy Christian smoking a cigarette in her white jade holder. Inez, wearing dark glasses (wearing dark glasses because, after four hours of sleep, a fight with Janet, and telephone calls from Carol Christian in San Francisco and Paul Christian in Suva, she had spent most of the day crying in her room: one last throe of her adolescence), pinning and repinning a gardenia in her damp hair. This is our niece, Inez, Dwight Christian said. Inez, Major Lovett. Jack. Inez, Mrs. Lovett. Carla. A breath of air, a cigarette. This champagne is lukewarm. One glass won't hurt you, Inez, it's your birthday. Inez's birthday.

Inez is seventeen. Inez's evening, really. Inez is our balletomane.

"Why are you wearing sunglasses," Jack Lovett said.

Inez Christian, startled, touched her glasses as if to remove them and then, looking at Jack Lovett, brushed her hair back instead, loosening the pins that held the gardenia.

Inez Christian smiled.

The gardenia fell to the wet grass.

"I used to know all the generals at Schofield," Cissy Christian said. "Great fun out there. Then."

"I'm sure." Jack Lovett did not take his eyes from Inez.

"Great polo players, some of them," Cissy Christian said. "I don't suppose you get much chance to play."

"I don't play," Jack Lovett said.

Inez Christian closed her eyes.

Carla Lovett drained her paper cup and crushed it in her hand.

"Inez is seventeen," Dwight Christian repeated.

"I think I want a real drink," Carla Lovett said.

During the days which immediately followed this meeting the image of Inez Christian was never entirely absent from Jack Lovett's mind, less a conscious presence than a shadow on the scan, an undertone. He would think of Inez Christian when he was just waking, or just going to sleep. He would summon up Inez

Christian during lulls in the waning argument he and
Carla Lovett were conducting that winter over when
or how or why she would leave him. His interest in
Inez was not, as he saw it, initially sexual: even at this
most listless stage of his marriage he remained com-
pelled by Carla, by Carla's very lethargy, and could
still be actively aroused by watching her brush out
her hair or pull on a shirt or kick off the huaraches she
wore instead of slippers.

What Jack Lovett believed he saw in Inez Christian
was something else. The picture he had was of Inez
listening to something he was telling her, listening
gravely, and then giving him her hand. In this picture
she was wearing the gardenia in her hair and the white
dress she had worn to the ballet, the only dress in
which he had ever seen her, and the two of them were
alone. In this picture the two of them were in fact the
only people on earth.

"Pretty goddamn romantic."

As Jack Lovett said to me on the Garuda 727 with
the jammed landing gear.

He remembered that her fingernails were blunt and
unpolished.

He remembered a scar on her left wrist, and how
he had wondered briefly if she had done it deliberately. He thought not.

It had occurred to him that he might never see her
again (given his situation, given her situation, given
the island and the fact that from her point of view he
was a stranger on it) but one Saturday night in Febru-

ary he found her, literally, in the middle of a cane-field; stopped to avoid hitting a stalled Buick on the narrow road between Ewa and Schofield and there she was, Inez Christian, age seventeen, flooding the big Buick engine while her date, a boy in a pink Oxford-cloth shirt, crouched in the cane vomiting.

They had been drinking beer, Inez Christian said, at a carnival in Wahiawa. There had been these soldiers, a bottle of rum, an argument over how many plush dogs had been won at the shooting gallery, the MPs had come and now this had happened.

The boy's name was Bobby Strudler.

Immediately she amended this: Robert Strudler.

The Buick belonged to Robert Strudler's father, she believed that the correct thing to do was to push the Buick onto a cane road and come out in daylight with a tow.

"The 'correct thing,' " Jack Lovett said. "You're a regular Miss Manners."

Inez Christian ignored this. Robert Strudler's father could arrange the tow.

She herself could arrange the tow.

In daylight.

Her feet were bare and she spoke even more precisely, as if to counter any suggestion that she might herself be drunk, and it was not until later, sitting in the front seat of Jack Lovett's car on the drive into town, Robert Strudler asleep in the back with his arms around the prize plush dogs, that Inez Christian gave any indication that she remembered him.

"I don't care about your wife," she said. She sat very straight and kept her eyes on the highway as she spoke. "So it's up to you. More or less."

She smelled of beer and popcorn and Nivea cream. The next time they met she had with her a key to the house on the Nuannu ranch. They had met a number of times before he told her that Carla Lovett had in fact already left him, had slept until noon on the last day of January and then, in an uncharacteristic seizure of hormonal energy, packed her huaraches and her shorty nightgowns and her Glenn Miller records and picked up a flight to Travis, and when he did tell her she only shrugged.

"It doesn't change anything," she said. "In point of fact."

In point of fact it did not, and it struck Jack Lovett then that what he had first read in Inez Christian as an extreme recklessness could also be construed as an extreme practicality, a temperamental refusal to deal with the merely problematic. The clandestine nature of their meetings was never questioned. The absence of any foreseeable future to these meetings was questioned only once, and that once by him.

"Will you remember doing this," Jack Lovett said.

"I suppose," Inez Christian said.

Her refusal to engage in even this most unspecific and pro forma speculation had interested him, even nettled him, and he had found himself persisting: "You'll go off to college and marry some squash player and forget we ever did any of it."

She had said nothing.

"You'll go your way and I'll go mine. That about it?"

"I suppose we'll run into each other," Inez Christian said. "Here or there."

By September of 1953, when Inez Christian left Honolulu for the first of the four years she had agreed to spend studying art history at Sarah Lawrence, Jack Lovett was in Thailand, setting up what later became the Air Asia operation. By May of 1955, when Inez Christian walked out of a dance class at Sarah Lawrence on a Tuesday afternoon and got in Harry Victor's car and drove down to New York to marry him at City Hall, with a jersey practice skirt tied over her leotard and a bunch of daisies for a bouquet, Jack Lovett was already in Saigon, setting up lines of access to what in 1955 he was not yet calling the assistance effort. In 1955 he was still calling it the insurgency problem, but even then he saw its possibilities. He saw it as useful. I believe many people did, while it lasted. "NOT A SQUASH PLAYER," Inez Christian wrote across the wedding announcement she eventually mailed to his address in Honolulu, but it was six months before he got it.

It occurs to me that for Harry Victor to have driven up to Sarah Lawrence on a Tuesday afternoon in May and picked up Inez Christian in her leotard and married her at City Hall could be understood as impulsive, perhaps the only thing Harry Victor ever did that might be interpreted as a spring fancy, but this interpretation would be misleading. There were practical factors involved. Harry Victor was due to start work in Washington the following Monday, and Inez Christian was two months pregnant.

The afternoon of the wedding was warm and bright.

Billy Dillon was the witness.

After the ceremony Inez and Harry Victor and Billy Dillon and a girl Billy Dillon knew that year rode the ferry to Staten Island and back, had dinner at Luchow's, and went uptown to hear Mabel Mercer at the RSVP.

In the spring of the year, Mabel Mercer sang, and *this will be my shining hour*.

Two months to the day after the wedding Inez miscarried, but by then Harry was learning the ropes at Justice and Inez had decorated the apartment in Georgetown (white walls, Harvard chairs, lithographs) and they were giving dinner parties, administrative assistants and *suprêmes de volaille à l'estragon* at the Danish teak table in the living room. When Jack Lovett finally got Inez's announcement he sent her a wedding present he had won in a poker game in Saigon, a silver cigarette box engraved *Résidence du Gouverneur Général de l'Indo-Chine*.

2

I N fact they did run into each other.

Here or there.

Often enough, during those twenty-some years during which Inez Victor and Jack Lovett refrained from touching each other, refrained from exhibiting undue pleasure in each other's presence or untoward interest in each other's activities, refrained most specifically from even being alone together, to keep the idea of it quick.

Quick, alive.

Something to think about late at night.

Something private.

She always looked for him.

She did not really expect to see him but she never got off a plane in certain parts of the world without wondering where he was, how he was, what he might be doing.

And once in a while he was there.

For example in Jakarta in 1969.

I learned this from her.

Official CODEL Mission, Dependents and Guests Accompanying, Inquiry into Status Human Rights in Developing (USAID Recipient) Nations.

One of many occasions on which Harry Victor

descended on one tropic capital or another and set about obtaining official assurance that human rights remained inviolate in the developing (USAID Recipient) nation at hand.

One of several occasions, during those years after Harry Victor first got himself elected to Congress, on which Inez Victor got off the plane in one tropic capital or another and was met by Jack Lovett.

Temporarily attached to the embassy.

On special assignment to the military.

Performing an advisory function to the private sector.

"Just what we need here, a congressman," Inez remembered Jack Lovett saying that night in the customs shed at the Jakarta airport. The customs shed had been crowded and steamy and it had occurred to Inez that there were too many Americans in it. There was Inez, there was Harry, there were Jessie and Adlai. There was Billy Dillon. There was Frances Landau, in the same meticulously pressed fatigues and French aviator glasses she had worn the year before in Havana. There was Janet, dressed entirely in pink, pink sandals, a pink straw hat, a pink linen dress with rickrack. "I thought pink was the navy blue of the Indies," Janet had said in the Cathay Pacific lounge at Hong Kong.

"India," Inez had said. "Not the Indies. India."

"India, the Indies, whatever. Same look, *n'est-ce pas?*"

"Possibly to you," Frances Landau said.

"What is that supposed to mean?"

"It means I don't quite see why you decided to get yourself up like an English royal touring the colonies."

Janet had assessed Frances Landau's fatigues, washed and pressed to a silvery patina, loose and seductive against Frances Landau's translucent skin.

"Because I didn't bring my combat gear," Janet had said then.

Inez did not remember exactly why Janet had been along (some domestic crisis, a ragged season with Dick Ziegler or a pique with Dwight Christian, a barrage of urgent telephone calls and a pro forma invitation), nor did she remember exactly under what pretext Frances Landau had been along (legislative assistant, official photographer, drafter of one preliminary report or another, the use of Bahasa Indonesian in elementary education on Sumatra, the effects of civil disturbance on the infrastructure left on Java by the Dutch), but there they had been, in the customs shed of the Jakarta airport, along with nineteen pieces of luggage and two book bags and two tennis rackets and the boogie boards that Janet had insisted on bringing from Honolulu as presents for Jessie and Adlai. Jack Lovett had picked up the tennis rackets and handed them to the embassy driver. "A tennis paradise here, you don't mind the ballboys carry submachine guns."

"Let's get it clear at the outset, I don't want this visit tainted," Harry Victor had said.

"No embassy orchestration," Billy Dillon said.

"No debriefing," Harry Victor said.

"No reporting," Billy Dillon said.

"I want it understood," Harry Victor said, "I'm promising unconditional confidentiality."

"Harry wants it understood," Billy Dillon said, "he's not representing the embassy."

Jack Lovett opened the door of one of the embassy cars double-parked outside the customs shed. "You're parading through town some night in one of these Detroit boats with the CD 12 plates and a van blocks you off, you just explain all that to the guys who jump out. You just tell them. They can stop waving their Uzis. You're one American who doesn't represent the embassy. That'll impress them. They'll back right off."

"There's a point that should be made here," Frances Landau said.

"Trust you to make it," Janet said.

Frances Landau ignored Janet. "Harry. Billy. See if you don't agree. The point—"

"They'll lay down their Uzis and back off saluting," Jack Lovett said.

"This sounds like something Frances will be dressed for," Janet said.

"—Point I want to make is this," Frances Landau said. "Congressman Victor isn't interested in confrontation."

"That's something else he can tell them." Jack Lovett was looking at Inez. "Any points you want to make? Anything you want understood? Mrs. Victor?"

"About this friend of Inez's," Frances Landau had said later that night at the hotel.

Inez was lying on the bed in the suite that had finally been found for her and Harry and the twins. There had been a mix-up about whether they were to stay at the hotel or at the ambassador's residence and when Harry had insisted on the hotel the bags had to be retrieved from the residence. "We always put Codels at the residence," the junior political officer had kept saying. "This Codel doesn't represent the embassy," Jack Lovett had said, and the extra rooms had been arranged at the desk of the Hotel Borobudur and Jack Lovett had left and the junior political officer was waiting downstairs for the bags with a walkie-talkie and one of the ten autographed paperback copies of *The View from the Street: Root Causes, Radical Solutions and a Modest Proposal* that Frances Landau had thought to bring in her carry-on bag.

"Which friend of Inez's exactly," Inez said.

"Jack whatever his name is."

"Lovett." Janet was examining the curtains. "His name is Jack Lovett. This is just possibly the ugliest print I have ever seen."

"Batik," Frances Landau said. "A national craft. Lovett then."

"Frances is so instructive," Janet said. "Batik. A national craft. There is batik and there is batik, Frances. For your information."

Frances Landau emptied an ice tray into a plastic bucket. "What does he do?"

Inez stood up. "I believe he's setting up an export-credit program, Frances." She glanced at Billy Dillon. "Operating independently of Pertamina."

"AID funding," Billy Dillon said. "Exploring avenues. Et cetera."

"So he said." Frances Landau dropped three of the ice cubes into a glass. "In those words."

"I thought he was in the aircraft business," Janet said. "Inez? Wasn't he? When he was married to Betty Bennett? I'd be just a little leery of those ice cubes if I were you, Frances. Ice cubes are not a national craft."

"Really, the aircraft business," Frances Landau said. "Boeing? Douglas? What aircraft business?"

"I wouldn't develop this any further, Frances," Harry Victor said.

"I'd definitely let it lie," Billy Dillon said. "In country."

"It's not that clear cut," Harry Victor said.

"But this is ludicrous," Frances Landau said.

"Not black and white," Harry Victor said.

"Pretty gray, actually," Billy Dillon said. "In country."

"But this is everything I despise." Frances Landau looked at Harry Victor. "Everything you despise."

Inez looked at Billy Dillon.

Billy Dillon shrugged.

"Harry, if you could hear yourself. 'Not that clear cut.' 'Not black and white.' That's not the Harry Victor I—"

Frances Landau broke off.

There was a silence.

"The four of you are really fun company," Janet said.

"This conversation," Frances Landau said, "is making me quite ill."

"That or the ice cubes," Janet said.

When Inez remembered that week in Jakarta in 1969 she remembered mainly the cloud cover that hung low over the city and trapped the fumes of sewage and automobile exhaust and rotting vegetation as in a fetid greenhouse. She remembered the cloud cover and she remembered lightning flickering on the horizon before dawn and she remembered rain washing wild orchids into the milky waste ditches.

She remembered the rumors.

There had been new rumors every day.

The newspapers, censored, managed to report these rumors by carrying stories in which they deplored the spreading of rumors, or, as the newspapers put it, the propagation of falsehoods detrimental to public security. In order to deplore the falsehoods it was of course necessary to detail them, which was the trick. Among the falsehoods deplored one day was a rumor that an American tourist had been killed in the rioting at Surabaya, the rioting at Surabaya being only another rumor, deplored the previous day. There was a further rumor that the *Straits Times* in Singapore was reporting not only an American tourist but also a German businessman killed, and rioting in Solo as well as in Surabaya, but even the existence of the

Straits Times report was impossible to confirm because the *Straits Times* was said to have been confiscated at customs. The rumor that the *Straits Times* had been confiscated at customs was itself impossible to confirm, another falsehood detrimental to public security, but there was no *Straits Times* in Jakarta for the rest of that week.

Inez remembered Harry giving a press conference and telling the wire reporters who showed up that the rioting in Surabaya reflected the normal turbulence of a nascent democracy.

Inez remembered Billy Dillon negotiating with the wire reporters to move Harry's press conference out in time for Friday deadlines at the New York *Times* and the Washington *Post*. "I made him available, now do me a favor," Billy Dillon said. "I don't want him on the wire so late he makes the papers Sunday afternoon, you see my point."

Inez remembered Jack Lovett asking Billy Dillon if he wanted the rioting rescheduled for the Los Angeles *Times*.

Inez remembered:

The reception for Harry at the university the night before the grenade exploded in the embassy commissary. She remembered Harry saying over and over again that Americans were learning major lessons in Southeast Asia. She remembered Jack Lovett saying finally that he could think of only one lesson Americans were learning in Southeast Asia. What was that, someone said. Harry did not say it, Harry was too careful to have said it. Billy Dillon was too careful to

99

have said it. Frances Landau or Janet must have said it. What was that, Frances Landau or Janet said, and Jack Lovett clipped a cigar before he answered.

"A tripped Claymore mine explodes straight up," Jack Lovett said.

There had been bare light bulbs blazing over a table set with trays of sweetened pomegranate juice, little gold chairs set in rows, some kind of trouble outside: troops appearing at the doors and the occasional crack of a rifle shot, the congressman says, the congressman believes, major lessons for Americans in Southeast Asia.

"Let's move it out," Jack Lovett said.

"Goddamnit I'm not through," Harry Victor said.

"I believe some human rights are being violated on the verandah," Jack Lovett said.

Harry had turned back to the director of the Islamic Union.

Janet's hand had hovered over the sweetened pomegranate juice as if she expected it to metamorphose into a vodka martini.

Inez had watched Jack Lovett. She had never before seen Jack Lovett show dislike or irritation. Dislike and irritation were two of many emotions that Jack Lovett made a point of not showing, but he was showing them now.

"You people really interest me," Jack Lovett said. He said it to Billy Dillon but he was looking at Harry. "You don't actually see what's happening in front of you. You don't see it unless you read it. You have to read it in the New York *Times*, then you start talking about it. Give a speech. Call for an investigation. Maybe you can come down here in a year or two, investigate what's happening tonight."

"You don't understand," Inez had said.

"I understand he trots around the course wearing blinders, Inez."

Inez remembered:

Jack Lovett coming to get them in the coffee shop of the Borobudur the next morning, after the grenade was lobbed into the embassy commissary. The ambassador, he said, had a bungalow at Puncak. In the mountains. Inez and Janet and the children were to wait up there. Until the situation crystallized. A few hours, not far, above Bogor, a kind of resort, he would take them up.

"A hill station," Janet said. "Divine."

"Don't call it a hill station," Frances Landau said. " 'Hill station' is an imperialist term."

"Let's save the politics until we get up there," Jack Lovett said.

"I don't want to go," Frances Landau said.

"Nobody gives a rat's ass if you go or don't go," Jack Lovett said. "You're not a priority dependent."

"Isn't this a little alarmist," Harry Victor said. Harry was cracking a boiled egg. Jack Lovett watched him spoon out the egg before he answered.

"This was a swell choice for a family vacation," Jack Lovett said then. "A regular Waikiki. I wonder why the charters aren't onto it. I also wonder if you know what it would cost us to get a congressman's kid back."

Jack Lovett's voice was pleasant, and so was Harry's.

"Ah," Harry said. "No. Not unless it's been in the New York *Times*."

Inez remembered:

The green lawn around the ambassador's bungalow at Puncak, the gardenia hedges.

The faded chintz slipcovers in the bungalow at Puncak, the English primroses, the tangles of bamboo and orchids in the ravine.

The mists blowing in at Puncak.

Standing with Jack Lovett on the green lawn at Puncak with the mists blowing in over the cracked concrete of the empty swimming pool, over the ravine, over the tangles of bamboo and orchids, over the English primroses.

Standing with Jack Lovett.

Inez remembered that.

Inez also remembered that the only person killed when the grenade exploded in the embassy commissary was an Indonesian driver from the motor pool. The news had come in on the radio at Puncak while Inez and Jack Lovett sat in the dark on the porch waiting for word that it was safe to take the children back down to Jakarta. There had been fireflies, Inez remembered, and a whine of mosquitoes. Jessie and Adlai were inside the bungalow trying to get Singapore television and Janet was inside the bungalow trying to teach the houseman how to make coconut milk punches. The telephones were out. The radio transmission was mainly static. According to the radio other Indonesian and American personnel had sustained minor injuries but the area around the embassy was secure. The ambassador was interviewed and expressed his conviction that the bombing of the embassy commissary was an isolated incident and did not reflect the mood of the country. Harry was interviewed and expressed his conviction that this isolated incident reflected only the normal turbulence of a nascent democracy.

Jack Lovett had switched off the radio.

For a while there had been only the whining of the mosquitoes.

Jack Lovett's arm was thrown over the back of his chair and in the light that came from inside the bungalow Inez could see the fine light hair on the back of his wrist. The hair was neither blond nor gray but was lighter than Jack Lovett's skin. "You don't understand him," Inez said finally.

"Oh yes I do," Jack Lovett said. "He's a congressman."

Inez said nothing.

The hair on the back of Jack Lovett's wrist was translucent, almost transparent, no color at all.

"Which means he's a radio actor," Jack Lovett said. "A civilian."

Inez could hear Janet talking to the houseman inside the bungalow. "I said coconut milk," Janet kept saying. "Not goat milk. I think you thought I said goat milk. I think you misunderstood."

Inez did not move.

"Who is Frances," Jack Lovett said.

103

Inez did not answer immediately. Inez had accepted early on exactly what Billy Dillon had told her: girls like Frances came with the life. Frances came with the life the way fundraisers came with the life. Sometimes fundraisers were large and in a hotel and sometimes fundraisers were small and at someone's house and sometimes the appeal was specific and sometimes the appeal was general but they were all the same. There was always the momentary drop in the noise level when Harry came in and there were always the young men who talked to Inez as a way of ingratiating themselves with Harry and there were always these very pretty women of a type who were excited by public life. There was always a Frances Landau or a Connie Willis. Frances Landau was a rich girl and Connie Willis was a singer but they were just alike. They listened to Harry the same way. They had the same way of deprecating their own claims to be heard.

It's just a means to an end, Frances said about her money.

I just do two lines of coke and scream, Connie said about her singing.

If there were neither a Frances nor a Connie there would be a Meredith or a Brooke or a Binky or a Lacey. Inez considered trying to explain this to Jack Lovett but decided against it. She knew about certain things that came with her life and Jack Lovett knew about certain things that came with his life and none of these things had any application to this moment on this porch. Jack Lovett reached for his seersucker jacket and put it on and Inez watched him. She could hear Janet telling Jessie and Adlai about the goat milk in the coconut milk punches. "It's part of the exaggerated politeness these people have," Janet said. "They'll never admit they didn't understand you. That would imply you didn't speak clearly, a no-no."

"Either that or he didn't have any coconut milk," Jack Lovett said.

Frances did not have any application to this moment on this porch and neither did Janet.

Inez closed her eyes.

"We should go back down," she said finally. "I think we should go back down."

"I bet you think that would be the 'correct thing,' " Jack Lovett said. "Don't you. Miss Manners."

Inez sat perfectly still. Through the open door she could see Janet coming toward the porch.

Jack Lovett stood up. "We've still got it," he said. "Don't we."

"Got what," Janet said as she came outside.

"Nothing," Inez said.

"Plenty of nothing," Jack Lovett said.

Janet looked from Jack Lovett to Inez.

Inez thought that Janet would tell her story about the coconut milk punches but Janet did not. "Don't you dare run off together and leave me in Jakarta with Frances," Janet said.

That was 1969. Inez Victor saw Jack Lovett only twice again between 1969 and 1975, once at a large party in Washington and once at Cissy Christian's funeral in Honolulu. For some months after the evening on the porch of the bungalow at Puncak it had seemed to Inez that she might actually leave Harry Victor, might at least separate herself from him in a provisional way—rent a small studio, say, or make a discreet point of not going down to Washington, and of being at Amagansett when he was in New York— and for a while she did, but only between campaigns.

Surely you remember Inez Victor campaigning.

Inez Victor smiling at a lunch counter in Manchester, New Hampshire, her fork poised over a plate of scrambled eggs and toast.

Inez Victor smiling at the dedication of a community center in Madison, Wisconsin, her eyes tearing in the bright sun because it had been decided that she looked insufficiently congenial in sunglasses.

Inez Victor speaking her famous Spanish at a street festival in East Harlem. *Buenos días,* Inez Victor said on this and other such occasions. *Yo estoy muy contenta a estar aquí hoy con mi esposo.* In twenty-eight states and at least four languages Inez Victor said that she was very happy to be here today with her husband. In twenty-eight states she also said, usually in English but in Spanish for *La Opinión* in Los Angeles and for *La Prensa* in Miami, that the period during which she and her husband were separated had been an important time of renewal and rededication for each of them (*vida nueva,* she said for *La Opinión,* which was not quite right but since the reporter was only humoring Inez by conducting the interview in

Spanish he got the drift) and had left their marriage stronger than ever. Oh shit, Inez, Jack Lovett said to Inez Victor in Wahiawa on the thirtieth of March, 1975. Harry Victor's wife.

3

AERIALISTS know that to look down
is to fall.

Writers know it too.

Look down and that prolonged spell of suspended
judgment in which a novel is written snaps, and re-
covery requires that we practice magic. We keep our
attention fixed on the wire, plan long walks, solitary
evenings, measured drinks at sundown and careful
meals at careful hours. We avoid addressing the thing
directly during the less propitious times of day. We
straighten our offices, arrange and rearrange certain
objects, talismans, props. Here are a few of the props
I have rearranged this morning.

Object (1): An old copy of *Who's Who*, open to
Harry Victor's entry.

Object (2): A framed cover from the April 21,
1975, issue of *Newsweek*, a black-and-white photograph showing the American ambassador to Cambodia,
John Gunther Dean, leaving Phnom Penh with the
flag under his arm. The cover legend reads "GETTING
OUT." There are several men visible in the background
of this photograph, one of whom I believe to be (the
background is indistinct) Jack Lovett. This photograph would have been taken during the period when

Inez Victor was waiting for Jack Lovett in Hong Kong.

Objects (3) and (4): two faded Kodacolor snapshots, taken by me, both showing broken rainbows on the lawn of the house I was renting in Honolulu the year I began making notes about this situation.

Other totems: a crystal paperweight to throw color on the wall, not unlike the broken rainbows on the lawn (dense, springy Bermuda grass, I remember it spiky under my bare feet) outside that rented house in Honolulu. A map of Oahu, with an X marking the general location of the same house, in the Kahala district, and red push-pins to indicate the locations of Dwight and Ruthie Christian's house on Manoa Road and Janet and Dick Ziegler's house on Kahala Avenue. A postcard I bought the morning I flew up from Singapore to see Inez Victor in Kuala Lumpur, showing what was then the new Kuala Lumpur International Airport at Subang. In this view of the Kuala Lumpur International Airport there are no airplanes visible but there is, suspended from the observation deck of the terminal, a banner reading "WELCOME PARTICIPANTS OF THE THIRD WORLD CUP HOCKEY." The morning I bought this postcard was one of several mornings, not too many, four or five mornings over a period of some years, when I believed I held this novel in my hand.

A few notes about those years.

The year I rented the house in Honolulu was 1975, in the summer, when everyone except Janet was still

109

alive and the thing had not yet congealed into a story on which the principals could decline comment. In the summer of 1975 each of the major and minor players still had a stake in his or her own version of recent events, and I spent the summer collecting and collating these versions, many of them conflicting, most of them self-serving; an essentially reportorial technique. The year I flew up to Kuala Lumpur to see Inez Victor was also 1975, after Christmas. I remember specifically that it was after Christmas because Inez devoted much of our first meeting to removing the silver tinsel from an artificial Christmas tree in the administrative office of the refugee camp where she then worked. She removed the tinsel one strand at a time, smoothing the silver foil with her thumbnail and laying the strands one by one in a shallow box, and as she did this she talked, in a low and largely uninflected voice, about certain problems Harry Victor was then having with the Alliance for Democratic Institutions. The Alliance for Democratic Institutions had originally been funded, Inez said, by people who wanted to keep current the particular framework of ideas, the particular political dynamic, that Harry Victor had come to represent (she said "Harry Victor," not "Harry," as if the public persona were an entity distinct from the "Harry" she later described as having telephoned her every night for the past week), but there had recently been an ideological rift between certain of the major donors, and this internal dissension was threatening the survival of the Alliance *per se.*

Inez smoothed another strand of tinsel and laid it in the box. The walls of the office were covered with charts showing the flow of refugees through the camp (or rather the flow of refugees into the camp, since many came but few left) and through an open door I could see an Indian doctor in the next room preparing to examine one of several small children. All of the children had bright rashes on their cheeks, and the little boy on the examining table, a child about four wearing an oversized sweatshirt printed OHIO WESLEYAN, intermittently cried and coughed, a harsh tubercular hack that cut through the sound of Inez's voice.

The Alliance *qua* Alliance.

Add to that the predictable difficulties of mobilizing broad-based support in the absence of the war.

Add further the usual IRS attempts to reverse the Alliance's tax-exempt status.

Add finally a definite perception that the idea of Harry Victor as once and future candidate had lost a certain momentum. Momentum was all in the perception of momentum. Any perception of momentum would naturally have suffered because of everything that happened.

I recall seizing on "everything that happened," thinking to guide Inez away from the Alliance for Democratic Institutions, but Inez could not, that first afternoon, be deflected. When the momentum goes, she said, by then plucking the last broken bits of tinsel from the artificial needles, the money goes with it.

The child on the examining table let out a piercing wail.

The Indian doctor spoke sharply in French and withdrew a hypodermic syringe.

Inez never looked up, and it struck me that I had been watching a virtually impenetrable performance. It was possible to construe this performance as not quite attached, but it was equally possible to construe it as deliberate, a studied attempt to deflect any idea I might have that Inez Victor would ever talk about how she left Honolulu with Jack Lovett.

4

I AM resisting narrative here.

Two documents that apply.

I was given a copy of the first by Billy Dillon in August of 1975, not in Honolulu but in New York, during the several days I spent there and on Martha's Vineyard talking to him and to Harry Victor.

UNIT ARRIVED AT LOCATION 7:32 AM 25 MARCH 1975. AT LOCATION BUT EXTERIOR TO RESIDENCE, OFFICERS NOTED AUTOMATIC GATE IN "OPEN" POSITION, AUTOMATIC SPRINKLERS IN OPERATION, AUTOMATIC POOL CLEANER IN OPERATION. OFFICERS NOTED TWO VEHICLES IN DRIVEWAY: ONE 1975 FORD LTD SEDAN (COLOR BLACK) BEARING HDMV PLATE "OYL-644" WITH US GOVERNMENT STICKER AND ONE 1974 MERCEDES 230-SL (COLOR LT. TAN) BEARING HDMV PLATE "JANET."

OFFICERS ENTERED RESIDENCE VIA OPEN DOOR, NOTED NO EVIDENCE OF DISARRAY OR STRUGGLE, AND PROCEEDED ONTO LANAI, THEREBY LOCATING FEMALE VICTIM LATER IDENTIFIED AS JANET CHRISTIAN ZIEGLER LYING FACE-DOWN ON CARPET. FEMALE VICTIM WAS POSITIONED ON CARPET NEAR LAVA-ROCK WALL LEADING TO SHALLOW POOL IN

113

WHICH OFFICERS OBSERVED ASSORTED PLANTINGS
AND KOI-TYPE FISH. FEMALE VICTIM WAS CLOTHED
IN LT. TAN SLACKS, WHITE BLOUSE, LT. TAN WIND-
BREAKER TYPE JACKET, NO STOCKINGS AND LOAFER
STYLE SHOES. A LEATHER SHOULDER STYLE PURSE
POSITIONED ON LEDGE OF LAVA-ROCK POOL CON-
TAINED FEMALE VICTIM'S IDENTIFICATION, AS-
SORTED CREDIT CARDS, ASSORTED PERSONAL ITEMS,
AND $94 CASH AND WAS APPARENTLY UNDISTURBED.

OFFICERS NOTED MALE VICTIM LATER IDENTIFIED
AS WENDELL JUSTICE OMURA LYING ON BACK NEAR
SOFA WITH APPARENT GUNSHOT WOUND UPPER AB-
DOMEN. MALE VICTIM WAS CLOTHED IN LT. TAN
SLACKS, ALOHA TYPE SHIRT, COTTON SPORTS JACKET,
WHITE SOCKS AND SNEAKER STYLE SHOES.

MALE VICTIM EXHIBITED NO PULSE RATE OR RE-
SPIRATORY ACTIVITY.

FEMALE VICTIM EXHIBITED LOW PULSE RATE
AND UNEVEN RESPIRATORY ACTIVITY.

AMBULANCE UNIT AND FIRE DEPARTMENT INHA-
LATOR SQUAD ARRIVED CONCURRENTLY AT 7:56 AM,
ALSO CONCURRENT WITH ARRIVAL OF MRS. ROSE L.
HAYAKAWA, 1173 21ST AVENUE, WHO IDENTIFIED
SELF AS REGULAR PARTTIME HOUSEKEEPER AND
STATED SHE LAST SAW FEMALE VICTIM PRECEDING
DAY AT 1 PM WHEN FEMALE VICTIM APPEARED IN
GOOD HEALTH AND SPIRITS. MRS. ROSE L. HAYAKAWA
STATED THAT SHE WAS FAMILIAR WITH MALE VIC-
TIM ONLY AS SPEAKER AT RECENT NISEI DAY BAN-
QUET HONORING ALL-OAHU HIGH-SCHOOL ATHLETES
OF JAPANESE DESCENT INCLUDING INFORMANT'S

SON DANIEL M. HAYAKAWA, SAME ADDRESS (NOT PRESENT AT LOCATION).

AMBULANCE CARRYING FEMALE VICTIM DISPATCHED TO QUEEN'S MEDICAL CENTER AT 8:04 AM.

APPARENT BLOODSTAINS REVEALED BY REMOVAL FEMALE VICTIM ALTERED SIGNIFICANTLY WHEN MRS. ROSE L. HAYAKAWA ATTEMPTED TO APPLY COLD WATER TO CARPET. OFFICERS PERSUADED MRS. ROSE L. HAYAKAWA TO TERMINATE THIS ATTEMPT.

MALE VICTIM PRONOUNCED DEAD AT LOCATION AND RESUSCITATION ATTEMPT TERMINATED AFTER ARRIVAL DEPUTY MEDICAL EXAMINER FLOYD LIU, M.D., AT 8:25 AM. REMOVAL OF BODY PENDING ARRIVAL INVESTIGATING OFFICERS AND OTHER MEDICAL EXAMINERS AT APPROXIMATELY 9 AM.

COPY TO: CORONER

COPY TO: HOMICIDE.

I was shown the second document, a cable transmitted from Honolulu on October 2, 1975, by its recipient, Inez Victor, when I saw her that December in Kuala Lumpur.

VICTORY STOP THINKING OF YOU IN OUR HOUR OF TRIUMPH STOP (SIGNATURE) DWIGHT.

Despite the signature this cable had been sent, Inez said, not by Dwight Christian but by her father, Paul Christian, on the morning he was formally committed in Honolulu to a state facility for the care and treatment of the insane.

5

I T was Billy Dillon who told Inez.

In the kitchen of the house at Amagansett.

To which he had driven, two hours in the rain on the Long Island Expressway and another hour on the Montauk Highway, flooding in the tunnel first shot out of the barrel and then construction on the L.I.E., no picnic, no day at the races, directly after he took the call from Dick Ziegler.

Dick Ziegler had called the office and tried to reach Harry.

Dick Ziegler was not yet on the scene, Dick Ziegler had been on Guam for two days trying to run an environmental-impact report around the Agana-Mariana Planning Commission.

Janet was not dead.

It was important to remember that Janet was not dead. Janet had been gravely injured, yes, in fact Janet was on life support at Queen's Medical Center, but Janet was not dead.

Wendell Omura was dead.

Inez must remember Wendell Omura, Inez would have met Wendell Omura in Washington, Wendell Omura was one of those Nisei who came out of the 442nd and went to law school on the G.I. Bill and spent the next twenty years cutting deals on a plane between Washington and his district. Silver Star. D.S.C. Real scrappy guy, had a triple bypass at Walter Reed a few years back, a week out of the hospital this spade tries to mug him, Omura decks the kid. The kind of guy who walks away from the Arno Line and a triple bypass, not to mention the spade, he probably didn't anticipate buying the farm on Janet's lanai.

Eating a danish.

Go for broke, see where it gets you.

The details were a little cloudy.

Don't ask, number one, how Wendell Omura happens to be on Janet's lanai.

Don't ask, number two, how Paul Christian happens to be seen leaving Janet's house with a .357 Magnum tucked in his beach roll.

The paper boy saw him.

The paper boy happened to recognize Paul Christian because Janet's paper boy is also Paul Christian's paper boy. Don't ask how the paper boy happened to recognize the .357 Magnum, maybe the paper boy is also a merc. There we are. Paul Christian has definitely been placed on the scene, but nobody can locate Paul Christian.

Paul Christian was the cloudy part.

Paul Christian was a fucking typhoon, you ask Billy Dillon.

Inez remembered listening to all this without speaking.

"I left word in Florida for Harry to call as soon as he checks in," Billy Dillon said. "Of course it's on the wire, but Harry might not hear the radio."

Inez lit a cigarette, and smoked it, leaning on the kitchen counter, looking out at the rain falling on the gray afternoon sea. Harry was on his way to Bal Harbour to speak at a Teamster meeting. Adlai was with Harry, earning credit for what the alternative college in Boston that had finally admitted him called an internship in public affairs. Jessie, at this hour in Seattle, would be just punching in at King Crab's Castle, punching in and putting on her apron and lining up the crab-cups-to-go, shredded lettuce, three fingers crab leg, King Crab's Special Sauce and lemon wedge on the side. Inez knew Jessie's exact routine at King Crab's Castle because Inez had spent Christmas with Jessie in Seattle. Jessie had cut her hair, gained ten pounds, and seemed, on methadone, generally cheerful.

"I was kind of thinking about going somewhere and getting a job," Jessie had said when Inez asked if she had given any thought to going back to school, possibly a class or two at NYU to start. "I understand there are some pretty cinchy jobs in Vietnam."

Inez had stared at her.

Jessie's information about the jobs in Vietnam was sketchy but she supposed that they involved "cooking for a construction crew, first aid, stuff like that."

Inez had tried to think about how best to phrase an objection.

"I got the idea from this guy I know who works for

Boeing, he hangs out at the Castle, you don't know him."

Inez had said in as neutral a voice as she could manage that she did not think Vietnam a good place to look for a job.

Jessie had shrugged.

"How's the junkie," Adlai had said when Inez walked back into the apartment on Central Park West a few days after Christmas.

"That's unnecessary," Harry had said.

Inez had not mentioned the jobs in Vietnam to either Harry or Adlai.

"Dick calls, he's still on Guam," Billy Dillon said. He had found a chicken leg in the refrigerator and was eating it. "He says he 'thinks' he can get a flight up to Honolulu tonight. I say what's to 'think' about, he says Air Micronesia's on strike and Pan Am and TW are booked but he's 'working on' a reservation. He's 'working on' a fucking reservation. A major operator, your brother-in-law. I said Dick, get your ass over to Anderson, the last I heard the Strategic Air Command still had a route to Honolulu. 'What do I say,' Dick says. 'Tell them your father-in-law offed a congressman.' 'Wait a minute, fella,' Dick says. 'Not so speedy.' He says, get this, direct quote, 'there's considerable feeling we can contain this to an accident.'"

Inez said nothing.

"It's Snow White and the Seven Loons down there.

119

'Contain this to an accident.' 'Considerable feeling.' Where's this 'considerable feeling' he's talking about? On Guam? I try to tell him, 'Dick, no go,' and Dick says 'why.' 'Why,' he says. A member of the Congress has been killed, Dick's own wife has been shot, his father-in-law's been fingered, his father-in-law who is also lest we forget the father-in-law of somebody who ran for president, and Dick's talking 'containment.' 'Dick,' I said, 'take it on faith, this one's a hang-out.' "

Inez said nothing. She had located a telephone number chalked on the blackboard above the telephone and begun to dial it.

"We're on the midnight Pan Am out of Kennedy. There's an hour on the ground at LAX which puts us down around dawn in Honolulu. I told Dick we wouldn't—"

Billy Dillon broke off. He was watching Inez dial.

"Inez," he said finally. "I can't help noticing you're dialing Seattle. I sincerely hope you're not calling Jessie. Just yet."

"Of course I am. I want to tell her."

"You don't think we've got enough loose balls on the table already? You don't think Jessie could wait until we line up at least one shot?"

"She'll read about it."

"Not unless it makes *Tiger Beat*."

"Don't say that. *Hello?*" Inez's voice was suddenly bright. "This is Inez Victor. Jessica Victor's mother. Jessie's mom, yes. I'm calling from New York. Amagansett, actually—"

"Oh good," Billy Dillon said. "Doing fine. Amagansett to King Crab."

"Jessie? Darling? Can you hear me? No, it's a little gray. Raining, actually. Listen. I—"

Inez suddenly thrust the receiver toward Billy Dillon.

"Never open with the weather," Billy Dillon said as he took the receiver. "Jessie? Jessie honey? Uncle William here. Your mother and I are flying down to Honolulu tonight, we wanted to put you in the picture, you got a minute? Well just tell the crab cups to stand easy, Jess, OK?"

"Oh shit," Billy Dillon said on the telephone in the Pan American lounge at the Los Angeles airport, when Dick Ziegler told him that Paul Christian had called the police from the Honolulu YMCA and demanded that they come get him. "Oh Jesus fucking Christ shit, I better let Harry know." By that time Harry Victor had already spoken to the Teamsters in Bal Harbour and was on his way to a breakfast meeting in Houston. Billy Dillon had hung up on Dick Ziegler and tried three numbers in Florida and five in Texas but Harry was somewhere in between and there was no time to wait because the flight was reboarding. "Oh shit," Billy Dillon kept saying all the way down the Pacific, laying out hand after hand of solitaire in the empty lounge upstairs. Inez lay on the curved banquette and watched him. Inez had watched

Billy Dillon playing solitaire on a lot of planes. "Why not trot out the smile and move easily through the cabin," he would say at some point in each flight, and the next day Inez would appear that way in the clips, the candidate's wife, "moving easily through the cabin," "deflecting questions with a smile."

"I have to admit I wasn't factoring in your father," Billy Dillon said now. "I knew he was a nutty, but I thought he was a nutty strictly on his own case. In fact I thought he was still looking for himself in Tangier. Or Sardinia. Or wherever the fuck he was when he used to fire off the letters to *Time* demanding Harry's impeachment."

"Tunis," Inez said. "He was in Tunis. He moved back to Honolulu last year. A mystic told him that Janet needed him. I told you. Listen. Do you remember before the Illinois primary when you and Harry and I were taken through the Cook County morgue?"

"Twenty-eight appearances in two days in Chicago and those clowns on advance commit us to a shake-hands with the coroner, very definitely I remember. Some metaphor. What about it."

"There was a noise in the autopsy room like an electric saw."

"Right."

"What was it?"

"It was an electric saw." Billy Dillon shuffled and cut the cards. "Don't dwell on it."

Inez said nothing.

"Don't anticipate. This one isn't going to improve, you try to look down the line. Think more like Jessie for once. I tell Jessie Janet's been shot, Janet's in a coma, we're not too sure what's going to happen, you know what Jessie says? Jessie says 'I guess whatever happens it's in her karma.' "

Inez said nothing.

"In . . . her . . . karma." Billy Dillon laid out another hand of solitaire. "That's the consensus from King Crab. Hey. Inez. Don't cry. Get some sleep."

"Watch the booze," Billy Dillon said about three A.M., and, a little later, to the stewardess who came upstairs and sat down beside him, "I'm only going to say this once, sweetheart, we don't want company." When first light came and the plane started its descent Billy Dillon reached across the table and took Inez's hand and held it. Inez had told Billy Dillon in Amagansett that there was no need for anyone to fly down with her but flying down with Inez was for Billy Dillon a reflex, part of managing a situation for Harry, and he held Inez's hand all the way to touchdown, which occurred at 5:37 A.M. Hawaiian Standard Time, March 26, 1975, on a runway swept by soft warm rain.

6

I WAS trained to distrust other people's versions, but we go with what we have.

We triangulate the coverage.

Handicap for bias.

Figure in leanings, predilections, the special circumstances which change the spectrum in which any given observer will see a situation.

Consider what filter is on the lens. So to speak. What follows is essentially through Billy Dillon's filter.

"This is a bitch," Billy Dillon remembered Dick Ziegler saying over and over. Dick Ziegler was still wearing the wrinkled cotton suit in which he had flown in from Guam and he was sitting on the floor in Dwight and Ruthie Christian's living room spreading shrimp paste on a cracker, covering the entire surface, beveling the edges.

Billy Dillon remembered the cracker particularly.

Billy Dillon could not recall ever before seeing a cracker given this level of attention.

"A real bitch. This whole deal. She was perfectly fine when I left for Guam."

"Why wouldn't she have been," Inez said.

Dick Ziegler did not look up. "She was going up to

San Francisco Friday. To see the boys. Chris and Timmy were coming up from school, she had it all planned."

"I mean it's not a lingering illness," Inez said. "Getting shot."

"Inez," Dwight Christian said. "See if this doesn't beat any martini you get in New York."

"You don't exhibit symptoms," Inez said.

"Inez," Billy Dillon said.

"I add one drop of glycerine," Dwight Christian said. "Old Oriental trick."

"She'd already made a dinner reservation," Dick Ziegler said. "For the three of them. At Trader's."

"You don't lose your appetite either," Inez said.

"Inez," Billy Dillon repeated.

"I heard you the first time," Inez said.

"What's the trouble here," Dick Ziegler said.

"About Wendell Omura," Inez said.

"Ruthie's on top of that." Dwight Christian seemed to have slipped into an executive mode. "Flowers to the undertaker. Something to the house. Deepest condolences. Tragic accident, distinguished service. Et cetera. Ruthie?"

"Millie's doing her crab thing." Ruthie began spreading crackers with the shrimp paste. "To send to the house."

"That's not just what I meant," Inez said.

"I hardly knew the guy, frankly," Dick Ziegler said. "On a personal basis."

"Somebody must have known him," Inez said. "On a personal basis."

Dwight Christian cleared his throat. "Adlai still a big Mets fan, Inez?"

Inez looked at Billy Dillon.

Billy Dillon stood up. "I think what Inez means—"

"Jessie still so horse crazy?" Ruthie Christian said.

"Horse crazy," Billy Dillon repeated. "Yes. She is. You could say that. Now. If I read Inez correctly— amend this if I'm off base, Inez—Inez is still just a little unclear about—"

Billy Dillon trailed off.

Now Ruthie Christian was arranging the spread crackers to resemble a chrysanthemum.

"This is a delicate area," Billy Dillon said finally.

Inez put down her glass. "Inez is still just a little unclear about what Wendell Omura was doing on Janet and Dick's lanai at seven in the morning," she said. "Number one. Number two—"

"Tell Jessie we've got a new Arabian at the ranch," Dwight Christian said. "Pereira blue mare, dynamite."

"—Two, Inez is still just a little unclear about what Daddy was doing on Janet and Dick's lanai with a Magnum."

"Your father wasn't seen on the lanai," Dick Ziegler said. "He was seen leaving the house. Let's keep our facts straight."

"Dick," Inez said. "He *said* he was on the lanai. He *said* he fired the Magnum. You know that."

There was a silence.

"You should get Inez to show you the ranch, Billy." Ruthie Christian did not look up. "Ask Millie to pack you a lunch, make a day of it."

"Number three," Inez said, "although less crucial, Inez is still just a little unclear about what Daddy was doing at the YMCA."

"If you drove around by the windward side you could see Dick's new project," Ruthie Christian said. "Sea Ranch? Sea Mountain? Whatever he calls it."

"He calls it Sea Meadow," Dwight Christian said. "Which suggests its drawback."

"Let's not get started on that," Dick Ziegler said.

"Goddamn swamp, as it stands."

"So was downtown Honolulu, Dwight. As it stood."

"Sea Meadow. I call that real truth-in-labeling. Good grazing for shrimp."

"Prime acreage, Dwight. As you know."

"Prime swamp. Excuse me. *Sacred* prime swamp. Turns out Dick's bought himself an old kahuna burial ground. Strictly *kapu* to developers."

"*Kapu* my ass. *Kapu* only after you started playing footsie with Wendell Omura."

"Speaking of Wendell Omura," Inez said.

"If you went around the windward side you could also stop at Lanikai." Ruthie Christian seemed oblivious, intent on her cracker chrysanthemum. "Give Billy a taste of how we really live down here."

"I think he's getting one now," Inez said.

Dwight Christian extracted the lemon peel from his martini and studied it.

Dick Ziegler gazed at the ceiling.

"Let's start by stipulating that Daddy was on the lanai," Inez said.

"Inez," Dwight Christian said. "I have thirty-two

127

lawyers on salary. In house. If I wanted to hear somebody talk like a lawyer, I could call one up, ask him
over. Give him a drink. Speaking of which—"

Dwight Christian held out his glass.

"Dwight's point as I see it is this," Ruthie Christian
said. She filled Dwight Christian's glass from the
shaker on the table, raised it to her lips and made a
moue of distaste. "Why air family linen?"

"Exactly," Dwight Christian said. "Why accentuate
the goddamn negative?"

"*Kapu* my ass," Dick Ziegler said.

Since Billy Dillon's filter tends to the comic his
memory may be broad. What he said some months
later about this first evening in Honolulu was that it
had given him a "new angle" on the crisis-management
techniques of the American business class. "They do
it with crackers," he said. "Old Occidental trick. All
the sharks know it." In his original account of that
evening and of the four days that followed Billy Dillon failed to mention Jack Lovett, which was his own
trick.

7

I ALSO have Inez's account.

Inez's account does not exactly conflict with Billy Dillon's account but neither does it exactly coincide. Inez's version of that first evening in Honolulu has less to do with those members of her family who were present than with those who were notably not.

Less to do with Dick Ziegler, say, than with Janet.

Less to do with Dwight and Ruthie Christian than with Paul Christian, and even Carol.

In Inez's version for example she at least got it straight about Paul Christian's room at the YMCA.

The room at the YMCA should have been an early warning, even Dick Ziegler and Dwight Christian could agree on that.

Surely one of them had told Inez before about her father's room at the YMCA.

His famous single room at the Y.

Paul Christian had taken this room when he came back from Tunis. He had never to anyone's knowledge spent an actual night there but he frequently mentioned it. "Back to my single room at the Y," he would say as he left the dinner table at Dwight and Ruthie's or at Dick and Janet's or at one or another house in Honolulu, and at least one or two of the other guests would rise, predictably, with urgent offers: a gate cottage here, a separate entrance there, the beach shack, the children's wing, absurd to leave it empty. Open the place up, give it some use. Doing us the favor, really. By way of assent Paul Christian would shrug and turn up his palms. "I'm afraid everyone knows my position," he would murmur, yielding.

Paul Christian had spoken often that year of his "position."

Surely Inez had heard her father speak of his position.

He conceived his position as "down," or "on the bottom," the passive victim of fortune's turn and his family's self-absorption ("Dwight's on top now, he can't appreciate my position," he said to a number of people, including Dick Ziegler), and, some months before, he had obtained the use of a house so situated—within sight both of Janet and Dick's house on Kahala Avenue and of the golf course on which Dwight Christian played every morning at dawn—as to exactly satisfy this conception.

"The irony is that I can watch Dwight teeing off while I'm making my instant coffee," he would sometimes say.

"The irony is that I can see Janet giving orders to her gardeners while I'm eating my little lunch of canned tuna," he would say at other times.

It was a location that ideally suited the prolonged mood of self-reflection in which Paul Christian arrived back from Tunis, and, during January and February, he had seemed to find less and less reason to leave the borrowed house. He had told several people that he was writing his autobiography. He had told others that he was gathering together certain papers that would constitute an indictment of the family's history in the islands, what he called "the goods on the Christians, let the chips fall where they may." He had declined invitations from those very hostesses (widows, divorcees, women from San Francisco who leased houses on Diamond Head and sat out behind them in white gauze caftans) at whose tables he was considered a vital ornament.

"I'm in no position to reciprocate," he would say if pressed, and at least one woman to whom he said this had told Ruthie Christian that Paul had made her feel ashamed, as if her very invitation had been presumptuous, an attempt to exploit the glamour of an impoverished noble. He had declined the dinner dance that Dwight and Ruthie Christian gave every February on the eve of the Hawaiian Open. He had declined at least two invitations that came complete with plane tickets (the first to a houseparty in Pebble Beach during the Crosby Pro-Am, the second to a masked ball at a new resort south of Acapulco), explaining that his sense of propriety would not allow him to accept first-class plane tickets when his position was such that he was reduced to eating canned tuna.

"Frankly, Daddy, everybody's a little puzzled by this 'canned tuna' business," Janet had apparently said one day in February.

"I'm sure I don't know why. Since 'everybody' isn't reduced to eating it."

"But I mean neither are you. Dwight says—"

"I'm sure it must be embarrassing for Dwight."

Janet had tried another approach.

"Daddy, maybe it's the 'canned' part. I mean what other kind of tuna is there?"

"Fresh. As you know. But that's not the point, is it."

"What is the point?"

"I'd rather you and Dwight didn't discuss my affairs, frankly. I'm surprised."

Tears of frustration would spring to Janet's eyes during these exchanges. "Canned tuna," she had said finally, "isn't even cheap."

"Maybe you could suggest something cheaper," Paul Christian had said. "For your father."

That was when Paul Christian had stopped speaking to Janet.

"Send him a whole tuna," Dwight Christian had advised when Janet reported this development. "Have it delivered. Packed in ice. Half a ton of bluefin. Goddamn, I'll do it myself."

Paul Christian had stopped speaking to Dwight a month before, after stopping by his office to say that the annual dinner dance on the eve of the Hawaiian Open seemed, from his point of view, a vulgar extravagance.

" 'Vulgar,' " Dwight Christian had repeated.

"Vulgar, yes. From my point of view."

"Why don't you say from the point of view of a Cambodian orphan?"

"I don't understand."

"I could see the point of view of a Cambodian orphan. I could appreciate this orphan's position on dinner dances in Honolulu. I might not agree wholeheartedly but I could respect it, I could—"

"You could what?"

As Dwight Christian explained it to Inez he had realized in that instant that this particular encounter was no-win. This particular encounter had been no-win from the time Paul Christian hit on the strategy of coming not to the house but to the office. He had come unannounced, in the middle of the day, and had been cooling his heels in the reception room like some kind of drill-bit salesman when Dwight Christian came back from lunch.

"Your brother's been waiting almost an hour," the receptionist had said, and Dwight had read reproach in her voice.

As tactics went this one had been minor but effective, a step up from turning down invitations on the ground that they could not be reciprocated, and its impact on Dwight Christian had been hard to articulate. Dwight Christian did not believe that he had mentioned it even to Ruthie. In fact he had pushed it from his mind. It had seemed absurd. In that instant in the office Dwight Christian had realized that Paul Christian was no longer presenting himself as the casual victim of his family's self-absorption. He was now presenting himself as the deliberate victim of his family's malice.

"I could buy the orphan's point of view," Dwight Christian had said finally. "I can't buy yours."

"Revealing choice of words."

Dwight Christian said nothing.

"Always trying to 'buy,' aren't you, Dwight?"

Dwight Christian squared the papers on his desk before he spoke. "Ruthie will miss you," he said then.

"I'm sure you can get one of your Oriental friends to fill out the table," Paul Christian said.

Later that day the receptionist had mentioned to the most senior of Dwight Christian's secretaries, who in due course mentioned it to him, that she found it "a little sad" that Mr. Christian's brother had to live at the YMCA.

That was January.

At first Dwight Christian said February but Ruthie corrected him: it would have been January because the invitations to the dance had just gone out.

The dance itself was February.

The Open was February.

In February there had been the dance and the Open and the falling-out with Janet over the canned tuna. In February there had also been the Chriscorp annual meeting, at which Paul Christian had embarrassed everyone, most especially (according to Ruthie) himself, by introducing a resolution that called for the company to "explain itself." Of course the newspapers had got hold of it. "Unspecified allegations flowed from one dissident family member but the votes were overwhelmingly with management at Chriscorp's annual meeting yesterday," the Honolulu *Advertiser* had read. "DISGRUNTLED CHRISTIAN SEEKS DISCLOSURE," was the headline in the *Star-Bulletin*.

The Chriscorp meeting was the fifteenth of February.

On the first of March Paul Christian had surfaced a second time in the *Advertiser*, with a letter to the editor demanding the "retraction" of a photograph showing Janet presenting an Outdoor Circle Environmental Protection Award for Special Effort in Blocking Development to Rep. Wendell Omura (D–Hawaii). Paul Christian's objection to the photograph did not appear to be based on the fact that the development Wendell Omura was then blocking was Dick Ziegler's. His complaint was more general, and ended with the phrase "lest we forget."

"I'm not sure they could actually 'retract' a photograph, Paul," Ruthie Christian had said when he called, at an hour when he knew Dwight to be on the golf course, to ask if she had seen the letter.

"I just want Janet to know," Paul Christian had said, "that in my eyes she's hit bottom."

He had said the same thing to Dick Ziegler. "An insult to you," he had added on that call. "How dare she."

"I respect your point," Dick Ziegler had said carefully, "but I wonder if the *Advertiser* was the appropriate place to make it."

"They've gone too far, Dickie."

After the letter to the *Advertiser* Paul Christian had begun calling Dick Ziegler several times a day with one or another cryptic assurance. "Our day's coming," he would say, or "tough times, Dickie, hang in there." Since it had been for Dick Ziegler a year of certain difficulties, certain reverses, certain differences with Dwight Christian (Dwight Christian's refusal to break ground for the mall that was to have been the linch-pin of the windward development was just one example) and certain strains with Janet (Janet's way of lining up with Dwight on the postponement of the windward mall had not helped matters), he could see in a general way that these calls from his father-in-law were intended as expressions of support.

Still, Dick Ziegler said to Inez, the calls troubled him.

He had found them in some way excessive.

He had found them peculiar.

"I may not be the most insightful guy in the world when it comes to human psychology," Dick Ziegler said, "but I think your dad went off the deep end."

"Fruit salad," Dwight Christian said.

"That's hindsight," Ruthie Christian said.

"What the hell does that mean?" Dwight Christian had stopped drinking martinis and lapsed into a profound irritability. "Of course it's hindsight. Jesus Christ. 'Hindsight.' "

"Janet loves you, Inez," Dick Ziegler said. "Don't ever forget that. Janet loves you."

8

Dᴜʀɪɴɢ the time I spent talking to Inez Victor in Kuala Lumpur she returned again and again to that first day in Honolulu. This account was not sequential. For example she told me initially, perhaps because I had told her what Billy Dillon said about the crackers, about talking to Dwight and Ruthie Christian and to Dick Ziegler, but it had been late in the day when she talked to Dwight and Ruthie Christian and to Dick Ziegler.

First there had been the hospital.

She and Billy Dillon had gone directly from the airport to the hospital but Janet was being prepared for an emergency procedure to drain fluid from her brain and Inez had been able to see her only through the glass window of the intensive care unit.

They had gone then to the jail.

"I suppose Dwight'll be breaking out the champagne tonight," Paul Christian had said in the lawyers' room at the jail.

Inez had looked at Billy Dillon. "Why," she said finally.

"You know." Paul Christian smiled. He seemed relaxed, even buoyant, tilting back his wooden chair

137

and propping his bare heels on the Formica table in the lawyers' room. His pants were rolled above his tanned ankles. His blue prison shirt was knotted jauntily at the waist. "You'll be there. I'm here. You can celebrate. Why not."

"Don't."

"Don't what? Actually I'm glad you're here." Paul Christian was still smiling. "I've been wondering what happened to Leilani Thayer's koa settee."

Inez considered this. "I have it in Amagansett," she said finally. "About Janet—"

"Strange, I didn't notice it when I visited you."

"You visited me in New York. The settee is in Amagansett. Daddy—"

"Not that I saw much of your apartment. The way I was rushed off to that so-called party."

Inez closed her eyes. Paul Christian had stopped in New York without notice in 1972, on his way back to Honolulu with someone he had met on Sardinia, an actor who introduced himself only as "Mark." *I can't fathom what you were thinking,* Paul Christian had written later to Inez, *when I brought a good friend to visit you and instead of welcoming the opportunity to know him better you dragged me off (altogether ignoring Mark's offer to do a paella, by the way, which believe me did not go unremarked upon) to what was undoubtedly the worst party I've ever been to where nobody made the slightest effort to communicate whatsoever . . .*

"Actually that wasn't a party," Inez heard herself saying.

"Inez," Billy Dillon said. "Wrong train."

"Not by any standard of mine," Paul Christian said. "No. It was certainly not a party."

"It wasn't meant to be. It was a fundraiser. You remember, Harry spoke."

"I do remember. I listened. Mr.—is it Diller? Dillman?"

"Dillon," Billy Dillon said. "On Track Two."

"Mr. Dillman here will testify to the fact that I listened. When your husband spoke. I also remember that not a soul I spoke to had any opinion whatsoever about what your husband said."

"You were talking to the Secret Service."

"Whoever. They all wore brown shoes. I'm surprised you have Leilani's settee. Since you never really knew her."

Billy Dillon looked at Inez. "Pass."

"Everyone called her 'Kanaka' when we were at Cal," Paul Christian said. "Kanaka Thayer."

Inez said nothing.

"She was a Pi Phi."

Inez said nothing.

"Leilani and I were like brother and sister. Parties night and day. Leilani singing scat. I was meant to marry her. Not your mother." He hummed a few bars of "The Darktown Strutters' Ball," then broke off. "I was considered something of a catch, believe it or not. Ironic, isn't it?"

Inez unfastened her watch and examined the face.

"My life might have been very different. If I'd married Leilani Thayer."

Inez corrected her watch from New York to Honolulu time.

"That settee always reminded me."

"I want you to have it," Inez said carefully.

"That's very generous of you, but no. No, thank you."

"I could have it shipped down."

"Of course you 'could.' I know you 'could.' That's hardly the point, you 'could,' is it?"

Inez waited.

"I'm through with all that," Paul Christian said.

Billy Dillon opened his briefcase. "You mean because you're here."

"That whole life," Paul Christian said. "The mission fucking children and their pathetic little sticks of bad furniture. Those mean little screens they squabble over. That precious settee you're so proud of. That's all bullshit, really. Third-rate. Pathetic. If you want to know the truth."

Billy Dillon took a legal pad from his briefcase. "I wonder if we could run through a few specifics here. Just a few details that might help establish—"

"And if you don't know what this did to me, Inez, making me beg for that settee—"

"—Establish a chronology—"

"—Humiliating me when I'm down—"

"—Times, movements—"

"—Then I'm sorry, Inez, I don't care to discuss it."

During the next half hour Billy Dillon had managed to elicit the following information. Some time between 6:45 and 7:10 the previous morning, from a position midway between the koi pool and the exterior door on Janet's lanai, Paul Christian had fired five rounds from the Smith & Wesson .357 Magnum he was carrying in his beach roll. He had then replaced the Magnum in the beach roll and made one call, not identifying himself, giving the police emergency operator Janet's address.

He had been aware that Wendell Omura was on the floor, yes.

He had also been aware that Janet was on the floor. Yes.

It would be quite impossible for either Inez or Mr. Dillman to understand how he felt about it.

When he left Janet's house he went not to the borrowed house in which he had been living but directly downtown to the YMCA. He had swum fifty laps in the YMCA pool, thirty backstroke and twenty Australian crawl.

"Be sure you put down 'crawl,' " he said. "I believe they call it 'freestyle' now but I'm sorry, I don't."

" 'Crawl,' " Billy Dillon said. "Yes."

After swimming Paul Christian had breakfasted on tea and yoghurt in the YMCA cafeteria. There had been "a little incident" with the cashier.

"What kind of incident," Billy Dillon said.

"Somebody says 'have a nice day' to me, I always say 'sorry, I've made other plans,' that usually puts them in their place, but not this fellow. 'You're quite a comedian,' this fellow says. Well, I just looked at him."

"That was the incident," Billy Dillon said.

"Someone speaks impertinently, you're better off not answering."

"I see," Billy Dillon said.

Paul Christian had gone then to his room, and spent the rest of the day packing the few belongings he kept there. He attached to each box a list of its contents. He made a master list indicating the disposition of each box. He wrote several letters, including one to Janet in which he explained that he "stood by his actions," and, early that evening, just before calling the police and identifying himself, left these letters and instructions for their delivery with the night clerk downstairs. There had been "a little incident" with the night clerk.

"He spoke impertinently," Billy Dillon said.

"Completely out of line. As were the police."

"The police were out of line."

"They treated me like a common criminal."

"Which you're not."

"Which I most assuredly am not. I told them. Just what I told Janet. I told them I stood by my actions."

"You told the police you stood by your actions."

"Absolutely."

"Just as you told Janet."

"Exactly." Paul Christian looked at Inez. "You're being very quiet."

Inez said nothing.

"Am I to interpret your silence as disapproval?"

Inez said nothing.

"Now that I'm jailed like a common criminal you're going to administer the coup de grace? Step on me?" Paul Christian turned back to Billy Dillon. "Janet and I have always been close. Not this one."

There was a silence.

"You're going to miss Janet," Billy Dillon said.

Paul Christian looked at Inez again. "I should have known you'd be down for the celebration," he said.

After Paul Christian was taken from the room Inez lit a cigarette and put it out before either she or Billy Dillon spoke. Billy Dillon was making notes on his legal pad and did not look up. "How about it," he said finally.

"Quite frankly I don't like crazy people. They don't interest me."

"That's definitely one approach, Inez." Billy Dillon put the legal pad into his briefcase and closed it. "Forthright. Hard-edge. No fuzzy stuff. But I think the note we want to hit today is a little further toward the more-in-sorrow end of the scale. Your father is 'a sick man.' He has 'an illness like any other.' He 'needs treatment.' "

"He needs to be put away."

"That's what we're calling 'treatment,' Inez. We're calling it 'treatment' when we talk to the homicide

guys and we're calling it 'treatment' when we talk to
the shrinks and we're calling it 'treatment' when we
talk to Frank Tawagata."

"I don't even know Frank Tawagata."

"You don't know the homicide guys, either, Inez.
Just pretend we're spending the rest of the day on
patrol. I'm on point." Billy Dillon looked at Inez.
"You all right?"

"Yes."

"Then trot out the smile and move easily through
the cabin, babe, OK?"

9

"**I** DON'T need to tell you, Frank, Harry appreciates what you did for him in Miami," Billy Dillon said at two o'clock that afternoon in Frank Tawagata's office. Billy Dillon and Inez had already seen the homicide detectives assigned to the investigation and they had already seen the psychiatrists assigned to examine Paul Christian and by then it was time to see Frank Tawagata. In fact Inez did know Frank Tawagata. She had met him at the 1972 convention. He had been a delegate. He was a lawyer, but his being a lawyer was not, Billy Dillon had said, the reason for seeing him. "This is a guy who truly believes, you want to get your grandma into heaven, you call in a marker at the courthouse," Billy Dillon had said. "Which is his strong point."

"You went to the wire for us in '72," Billy Dillon said now. "Harry knows that."

"Harry did one or two things for Wendell." Frank Tawagata did not look at Inez. "Anything I did for Harry I did for Wendell. Strictly."

"Harry knows that. Harry appreciates your position. Push comes to shove, you're on Wendell's team here. Which is why we're not pushing, Frank. You

talk to Harry or me, you're talking *in camera*.
Strictly."

"Strictly *in camera*," Frank Tawagata said, "I still
can't help you."

"You can't, you can't. Just say the word."

"I just said it."

Inez watched Billy Dillon. She was tired. She had
not eaten since breakfast the day before in Amagansett. She did not know what it was that Billy Dillon
wanted from Frank Tawagata but she knew that he
would get it. She could tell by the slight tensing of his
shoulders, the total concentration with which he had
given himself over to whatever it was he wanted.

"Wendell was a very well-liked guy," Billy Dillon
said. "In the community. I know that."

"Very well-liked."

"Very respected family. The Omuras. Locally."

"Very respected."

"Not unlike the Christians. Ironic." Billy Dillon
looked out the window. "One of the Omuras is even
involved with Dwight Christian, isn't he? Via Wendell? Some kind of business deal? Some trade-off or
another?"

Frank Tawagata had not answered immediately.

Billy Dillon was still looking out the window.

"I wouldn't call it a trade-off," Frank Tawagata
said then.

"Of course you wouldn't, Frank. Neither would I."

There was a silence.

"Wasn't your wife an Omura?" Billy Dillon said.
"Am I wrong on that?"

"No," Frank Tawagata said after a slight pause.

"Your wife wasn't an Omura?"

"I meant no, you're not wrong."

Billy Dillon smiled.

"So there would be a definite conflict," Frank Tawagata said, "if you were asking me to work on the defense."

"We're not talking 'defense,' Frank. We're talking a case that shouldn't see trial."

"I see."

"We're talking a sick man. Who needs help." Billy Dillon glanced at Inez. "Who needs treatment. And is going to get it."

"I see," Frank Tawagata said. "Yes."

"Look. Frank. All we need from you is a reading. A reading on where the markers are, what plays to expect. You know the community. You know the district attorney's office."

Frank Tawagata said nothing.

"I wouldn't think there was anybody shortsighted enough to see a career in playing this out in the media, but I don't know the office. For all I know, there's some guy over there operating in the bozo zone. Some guy who thinks he can make a name going to trial, embarrassing the Christians."

Frank Tawagata said nothing.

"Embarrassing Harry. Because face it, the guy to get is Harry."

"I would say 'was' Harry."

"Run that down for me."

"Harry's already been got, hasn't he? In '72?"

147

"Free shot, Frank. You deserve it. One of Wendell's cousins, isn't it? This deal with Dwight Christian?"

Frank Tawagata picked up a silver pen from his desk and poised it between his index fingers.

Inez watched Billy Dillon's shoulders. Killer mick, Harry always said about Billy Dillon, an accolade.

Billy Dillon leaned forward almost imperceptibly.

It occurred to Inez that the reason Harry was not himself a killer was that he lacked the concentration for it. Some part of his attention was always deflected back toward himself. A politician, Jack Lovett had said at Puncak. A radio actor.

"Didn't I see something about this in *Business Week?*" Billy Dillon said. "Just recently? Something about the container business? Is that right? One of Wendell's cousins?"

"One of Wendell's brothers." Frank Tawagata replaced the pen in its onyx holder before he spoke again. "My wife is a cousin."

"There you go," Billy Dillon said. "I love a town this size."

By three o'clock that afternoon it had been agreed, and could be duly reported to Harry Victor, that Frank Tawagata would sound out the district attorney's office on the most discreet and expeditious way to handle the eventual commitment to treatment of Paul Christian.

It had been agreed that Frank Tawagata would

discuss the advisability of this disposition with certain key elements in the Nisei political community.

It had been agreed that Frank Tawagata would make his special understanding of both the district attorney's office and the community available to whatever lawyer was chosen to represent Paul Christian at what would ideally be mutually choreographed proceedings.

"You're not visualizing a criminal specialist," Frank Tawagata said.

"I'm visualizing a goddamn trust specialist," Billy Dillon said. "One of the old-line guys. One of those guys who's not too sure where the crapper is in the courthouse. I told you. We're not mounting a criminal defense here."

All that had been agreed upon and it had been agreed, above all, that no purpose would be served by further discussion of why Wendell Omura had introduced legislation hindering the development of Dick Ziegler's Sea Meadow, of how that legislation might have worked to benefit Dwight Christian, or of what interest Wendell Omura's brother might recently have gained in the Chriscorp Container Division.

"How exactly did you know that," Inez said when she and Billy Dillon left Frank Tawagata's office.

"Just what I said. *Business Week*. Something I read on the plane coming down."

"About Dwight?"

"Not specifically."

"About Dick?"

"About some Omura getting into containers. Two lines. A caption. That's all."

"You didn't even know it was Wendell Omura's brother?"

"I knew his name was Omura, didn't I?"

"Omura is a name like Smith."

"Inez, you don't get penalties for guessing," Billy Dillon said. "You know the moves."

10

B y the time Inez and Billy Dillon got back to Queen's Medical Center that first day in Honolulu it was almost four o'clock, and Janet's condition was unchanged. According to the resident in charge of the intensive care unit the patient was not showing the progress they would like to see. The patient's body temperature was oscillating. That the patient's body temperature was oscillating suggested considerable brainstem damage.

The patient was not technically dead, no.

The patient's electroencephalogram had not even flattened out yet.

Technical death would not occur until they had not one but three flat electroencephalograms, consecutive, spaced eight hours apart.

That was technical death, yes.

"Technical as opposed to what?" Inez said.

The resident seemed confused. "What we call technical death is death, as, well—"

"As opposed to actual death?"

"As opposed to, well, not death."

"Technical life? Is that what you mean?"

"It's not necessarily an either-or situation, Mrs. Victor."

"Life and death? Are not necessarily either-or?"

"Inez," Billy Dillon said.

"I want to get this straight. Is that what he's saying?"

"I'm saying there's a certain gray area, which may or may not be—"

Inez looked at Billy Dillon.

"He's saying she won't make it," Billy Dillon said.

"That's what I wanted to know."

Inez stood by the metal bed and watched Janet breathing on the respirator.

Billy Dillon waited a moment, then turned away.

"She called me," Inez said finally. "She called me last week and asked me if I remembered something. And I said I didn't. But I do."

When Inez talked to me in Kuala Lumpur about seeing Janet on the life-support systems she mentioned several times this telephone call from Janet, one of the midnight calls that Janet habitually made to New York or Amagansett or wherever Inez happened to be.

Do you remember, Janet always asked on these calls.

Do you remember the jade bat Cissy kept on the hall table. The ebony table in the hall. The ebony table Lowell Frazier said was maple veneer painted black. But you can't have forgotten Lowell Frazier, you have to remember Cissy going through the roof when Lowell and Daddy went to Fiji together. The time Daddy wanted to buy the hotel. Inez, the ten-room hotel. In Suva. After Mother left. Or was it before? You must remember. Concentrate. Now that I have you. I'm frankly amazed you picked up the telephone, usually you're out. I'm watching an absolutely paradisical sunset, how about you?

"It's midnight here," Inez had said on this last call from Janet.

"I dialed, and you picked up. Amazing. Usually I get your service. Now. Concentrate. I've been thinking about Mother. Do you remember Mother crying upstairs at my wedding?"

"No," Inez had said, but she did.

On the day Janet married Dick Ziegler at Lanikai Carol Christian had started drinking champagne at breakfast. She had a job booking celebrities on a radio interview show in San Francisco that year, and by noon she was placing calls to entertainers at Waikiki hotels asking them to make what she called guest appearances at Janet's wedding.

As you may or may not remember I'm the mother of the bride, Carol Christian said by way of greeting people at the reception.

I'd pace my drinks if I were you, Paul Christian had said.

I should worry, I should care, Carol Christian sang with the combo that played for dancing on the deck a Chriscorp crew had just that morning laid on the beach.

Your mother's been getting up a party for the Rose Bowl, Harry Victor said.

Carol's a real pistol, Dwight Christian said.

153

I should marry a millionaire.

It was when Janet went upstairs to change out of her white batiste wedding dress that Carol Christian began to cry. Not to blame your Uncle Dwight, she kept repeating, sitting on the bed in which she had fifteen years before taken naps with Inez and Janet. Our best interests at heart. Not his fault. Your grandmother. Cissy. Really. Too much. Anyhow, anyhoo. All's well that ends in bed. Old San Francisco saying. I got my marvelous interesting career, *which* I never would have had, and you got—

Inez, heavily pregnant that year, sat on the bed and tried to comfort her mother.

We got married, Janet prompted.

Forget married, Carol Christian said. You got horses. Convertibles when the time came. Tennis lessons.

I couldn't have paid for stringing your rackets if I'd taken you with me.

Let alone the lessons.

Forget the little white dresses.

Never mind the cashmere sweater sets and the gold bracelets and the camel's-hair coats.

I beg to differ, Janet Christian, Mrs. Ziegler, you did so have a camel's-hair coat.

You wore it when you came up for Easter in 1950.

Mon cher Paul: Who do you f—— to get off this island? (Just kidding of course) XXXX, C.

Neither Inez nor Janet had spoken. The windows were all open in the bedroom and the sounds of the party drifted upstairs in the fading light. Down on the beach the bridesmaids were playing volleyball in their gingham dresses. The combo was playing a medley from *My Fair Lady*. Brother Harry, Inez heard Dick Ziegler say directly below the bedroom windows. Let the man build you a real drink.

Where's Inez, Harry Victor said. I don't want Inez exhausted.

Enough of the bubbly, time for the hard stuff, Dick Ziegler said.

Excuse me but I'm looking for my wife, Harry Victor said.

Whoa man, excuse me, Dick Ziegler said. I doubt very much she's lost.

Upstairs in the darkening bedroom Janet had taken off her stephanotis lei and placed it on their mother's shoulders.

I should worry, I should care.
I should marry a millionaire.

Inez did remember that.

Inez also remembered that when she and Janet were fourteen and twelve Janet had studied snapshots of Carol Christian and cut her hair the same way.

Inez also remembered that when she and Janet were fifteen and thirteen Janet had propped the postcards from San Francisco and Lake Tahoe and Carmel against her study lamp and practiced Carol Christian's handwriting.

"Partners in a surprisingly contemporary marriage in which each granted the other freedom to pursue wide-ranging interests," was how Billy Dillon had solved the enigma of Paul and Carol Christian for Harry Victor's campaign biography. The writer had not been able to get it right and Billy Dillon had himself devised this slant.

Aloha oe.

I believe your mother wants to go to night clubs.

Nineteen days after Janet's wedding Carol Christian had been dead, killed in the crash of a Piper Apache near Reno, and there in the third-floor intensive care unit at Queen's Medical Center Janet was about to be dead. Janet had asked Inez to remember and Inez had pretended that she did not remember and now Janet had moved into the certain gray area between either and or.

Aloha oe.

Inez had touched Janet's hand, then turned away.

The click of her heels on the hospital floor struck her as unsynchronized with her walk.

The sound of her voice when she thanked the resident struck her as disembodied, inappropriate.

Outside the hospital rain still fell, and traffic was backed up on the Lunalilo Freeway. On the car radio there was an update on Janet's guarded condition at Queen's Medical Center, and on the numbers of congressmen and other public officials who had sent wires and taped messages expressing their sympathy and deep concern about the death of Wendell Omura. Among the taped messages was one from Harry, expressing not only his sympathy and deep concern but his conviction that this occasion of sadness for all Americans could be an occasion of resolve as well (Inez recognized Billy Dillon's style in the balanced "occasions"), resolve to overcome the divisions and differences tragically brought to mind today by this incident in the distant Pacific.

"Not so distant you could resist a free radio spot," Inez said to Billy Dillon.

At five o'clock that afternoon, when Inez and Billy Dillon arrived at Dwight and Ruthie Christian's house, the first thing Inez noticed was a photograph on the hall table of Janet, a photograph taken the day Janet married Dick Ziegler, Janet barefoot on the beach at Lanikai in her white batiste wedding dress. The photograph did not belong on the hall table, which was why Inez noticed it. The photograph had always been on Ruthie Christian's dressing table, and now it was here, its silver frame recently polished, the table on which it sat recently cleared of car keys and scarves and lacquer boxes and malachite frogs. The photograph was an offering, a propitiatory message to an indefinite providence, and the message it confirmed was that Janet was available to be dead.

"I called St. Andrew's this morning and told Chip Kinsolving what we want," Dwight Christian was saying in the living room. "When the time comes. Just the regular service, in and out, the ashes to ashes business. And maybe a couple of what do you call them, psalms. Not the one about the Lord is my goddamn shepherd. Specifically told him that. Dick? Isn't that what you want?"

"Don't anticipate," Dick Ziegler said. "How do I know what I want. She's not dead."

"Passive crap, the Lord is my shepherd," Dwight Christian said. "No sheep in this family."

157

"I'll tell you what I want," Inez heard herself say as she walked down the few steps into the living room. She was remotely aware, as if through Demerol, of the vehemence in her voice. "I want you to put that picture back where it belongs."

At this moment when Inez Victor walked into the living room of the house on Manoa Road she was still wearing the short knitted skirt and the cotton jersey and the plumeria lei in which she had left the airport ten hours before.

She had not yet slept.

She had not yet eaten.

She had not yet seen Jack Lovett, although Jack Lovett had seen her.

Get her in out of the goddamn rain, Jack Lovett had said.

11

Tʜɪs much is now known about how Jack Lovett had spent the several months which preceded Inez Victor's arrival in Honolulu: he had spent those months shuttling between Saigon and Hong Kong and Honolulu. There had been innumerable details, loose ends, arrangements to be made. There had been exit paperwork to be fixed. There had been cash to be transferred. There had been end-user certificates to be altered for certain arms shipments, entry visas to be bought, negotiations to be opened and contacts to be made and houses to be located for displaced Vietnamese officers and officials (even this most minor detail was delicate, in those months when everyone knew the war was ending but everyone pretended that it was not, and Jack Lovett handled such purchases himself, with cash and the mention of overseas associates); the whole skein of threads necessary to transfer the phantom business predicated on the perpetuation of the assistance effort. That there is money to be made in time of war is something we all understand abstractly. Fewer of us understand war itself as a specifically commercial enterprise, but Jack Lovett did, not abstractly but viscerally, and his overriding concern during the months before Inez Victor reentered the field of his direct vision (she had always been there in his peripheral vision, a fitful shadow, the image that came forward when he was alone in a hotel room or at 35,000 feet) had been to insure the covert survival of certain business interests. On the morning Jack Lovett watched Inez arrive at the Honolulu airport, for example, he also watched the arrival and clearance from Saigon and immediate transshipment to Geneva via Vancouver of a certain amount of gold bullion, crated and palleted as "household effects." When he later mentioned this gold bullion to Inez he described it as "a favor I did someone." Jack Lovett did many people many favors during the spring of 1975, and many people did Jack Lovett favors in return.

As a reader you are ahead of the narrative here.

As a reader you already know that Inez Victor and Jack Lovett left Honolulu together that spring. One reason you know it is because I said so, early on. Had I not said so you would have known it anyway: you would have guessed it, most readers being rather quicker than most narratives, or perhaps you would even have remembered it, from the stories that appeared in the newspapers and on television when Jack Lovett's operation was falling apart.

You might even have seen the film clip I mentioned.

Inez Victor dancing on the St. Regis Roof.

Nonetheless.

I could still do Inez Victor's four remaining days

in Honolulu step by step, could proceed from the living room of the house on Manoa Road into the dining room and tell you exactly what happened that first night in Honolulu when Inez and Billy Dillon and Dick Ziegler and Dwight and Ruthie Christian finally sat down to dinner.

I could give you Jack Lovett walking unannounced into the dining room, through the French doors that opened onto the swimming pool.

I could give you Inez looking up and seeing him there.

"Goddamn photographers camped on the front lawn," Dwight Christian would say. "Jack. You know Inez. You know Janet's husband. Dick. You know Billy here?"

"We were both in Jakarta a few years back." Jack Lovett would be speaking to Dwight Christian but looking at Inez. "Inez was there. Inez was in Jakarta with Janet."

"Inez was also in Jakarta with her husband." Billy Dillon's voice would be pleasant. "And her two children."

"The reason the vultures are on the lawn is this," Dwight Christian would say. "Janet's not cutting it."

"Don't talk about Janet 'not cutting it,'" Dick Ziegler would say. "Don't sit there eating chicken pot pie and talk about Janet 'not cutting it.'"

"A change of subject," Dwight Christian would say. "For Dick. While I finish my chicken pot pie. Jack. What would you say if I told you Chriscorp was bidding a complete overhaul at Cam Ranh Bay?"

"I'd say Chriscorp must be bidding it for Ho Chi Minh." Jack Lovett would still look only at Inez. "How are you."

Inez would say nothing, her eyes on Jack Lovett.

"Do you want to go somewhere," Jack Lovett would say, his voice low and perfectly level.

A silence would fall over the table.

Inez would pick up her fork and immediately lay it down.

"Millie has dessert," Ruthie Christian would say, faintly.

"Inez," Billy Dillon would say.

Jack Lovett would look away from Inez and at Billy Dillon. "Here it is," he would say in the same low level voice. "I don't have time to play it out."

Well, there you are.

I could definitely do that.

I know the conventions and how to observe them, how to fill in the canvas I have already stretched; know how to tell you what he said and she said and know above all, since the heart of narrative is a certain calculated ellipsis, a tacit contract between writer and reader to surprise and be surprised, how not to tell you what you do not yet want to know. I appreciate the role played by specificity in this kind of narrative: not just the chicken pot pie and not just the weather either (I happen to like weather, but weather is easy), not just the way the clouds massed on the Koolau Range the next morning and not just the clatter of the palms in the afternoon trades behind Janet's house (anyone can do palms in the afternoon trades) when Inez went to get the dress in which Janet was buried.

I mean more than weather.

I mean specificity of character, of milieu, of the apparently insignificant detail.

The fact that when Harry and Adlai Victor arrived in Honolulu on the morning of March 28, Good Friday morning, the morning Janet's body was delivered to the coroner for autopsy, they were traveling on the Warner Communications G-2. The frequent occasions over the long Easter weekend before Janet's funeral on which Adlai found opportunity to mention the Warner Communications G-2. The delicacy of reasoning behind the decision that Harry and Adlai, but not Inez, should call on Wendell Omura's widow. The bickering over the arrangements for Janet's funeral (Dick Ziegler did after all want the Lord as Janet's shepherd, if only because Dwight Christian did not), and the way in which Ruthie Christian treated the interval between Janet's death and Janet's funeral as a particularly bracing exercise in quartermastering. The little flare-up when Inez advised Dick Ziegler that he could not delegate to Ruthie the task of calling Chris and Timmy at school to tell them their mother was dead.

"Frankly, Inez, when it comes to handling kids, I don't consider you the last word," Dick Ziegler said. "Considering Jessie."

"Never mind Jessie," Inez said. "Make the call."

The little difficulty Saturday morning when Chris

and Timmy flew in from school and the airport dogs picked up marijuana in one of their duffels. The exact text of the letter Paul Christian drafted to the *Advertiser* about the "outrage" of not being allowed to attend Janet's funeral. The exact location of the arcade in Waianae where Jack Lovett took Inez to meet the radar specialist who was said to have seen Jessie.

Jessie.

Jessie is the crazy eight in this narrative.

I plan to address Jessie presently, but I wanted to issue this warning first: like Jack Lovett and (as it turned out) Inez Victor, I no longer have time for the playing out.

Call that a travel advisory.

A narrative alert.

12

THE first electroencephalogram to show the entirely flat line indicating that Janet had lost all measurable brain activity was completed shortly before six o'clock on Wednesday evening, March 26, not long after Inez and Billy Dillon arrived at the house on Manoa Road. This electroencephalogram was read by the chief neurologist on Janet's case at roughly the time Inez and Billy Dillon and Dick Ziegler and Dwight and Ruthie Christian sat down to the chicken pot pie. The neurologist notified the homicide detectives that the first flat reading had been obtained, called the house on Manoa Road in an effort to reach Dick Ziegler, got a busy signal, and left the hospital, leaving an order with the resident on duty in the unit to keep trying Dick Ziegler. Ten minutes later a felony knifing came up from emergency and the resident overlooked the order to call Dick Ziegler.

This poses one of those questions that have to do only with perceived motive: would it have significantly affected what happened had the call come from the hospital before Inez got up from the dinner table and walked through the living room and out the front door with Jack Lovett? I think not, but a call

165

from the hospital could at least have been construed as the "reason" Inez left the table.

A reason other than Jack Lovett.

A reason they could all pretend to accept.

As it was they could pretend only that Inez was overwrought. Ruthie Christian was the first to locate this note. "She's just overwrought," Ruthie Christian said, and Billy Dillon picked it up: "Overwrought," he repeated. "Absolutely. Naturally. She's over-wrought."

As it was Inez just left.

"You could probably take off the lei," Jack Lovett said when they were sitting in his car outside the house on Manoa Road. Most of the reporters on the lawn seemed to have gone. There had been a single cameraman left on the steps when Inez and Jack Lovett came out of the house and he had perfunctorily run some film and then retreated. Jack Lovett had twice turned the ignition on and twice turned it off.

Inez took the crushed lei from around her neck and dropped it on the seat between them.

"I don't know where I thought we'd go," Jack Lovett said. "Frankly."

Inez looked at Jack Lovett and then she began to laugh.

"Hell, Inez. How was I to know you'd come?"

"You've had twenty years. To think where we'd go."

"Well sure. Stop laughing. I used to think I could always take you to Saigon. Drink citron pressé and watch the tennis. Scratch that. You want to go to the hospital?"

"Pretend we did go to Saigon. Pretend we did it all. Imagine it. It's all in the mind anyway."

"Not entirely," Jack Lovett said.

Inez looked at him, then away. The cameraman on the steps lit a cigarette and immediately flicked it across the lawn. He picked up his minicam and started toward the car. Inez picked up the lei and dropped it again. "Are we going to the hospital or not," she said finally.

Which was how Inez Victor and Jack Lovett happened to walk together into the third-floor intensive care unit at Queen's Medical Center when, as the older of the two homicide detectives put it, Janet's clock was already running.

"But I don't quite understand this," Inez kept saying to the resident and the two homicide detectives. The homicide detectives were at the hospital only to get a statement from one of the nurses and they wanted no part of Inez's interrogation of the resident. "You got a flat reading at six o'clock. Isn't that what you said?"

"Correct."

"And you need three. Eight hours apart. Isn't that what you told me? This afternoon? About technical death?"

"Also correct." The resident's face was flushed with irritation. "At least eight hours apart."

"Then why are you telling me you scheduled the second electroencephalogram for nine tomorrow morning?"

"At *least* eight hours apart. At least."

"Never mind 'at least.' You could do it at two this morning."

"That wouldn't be normal procedure."

Inez looked at the homicide detectives.

The homicide detectives looked away.

Inez looked at Jack Lovett.

Jack Lovett shrugged.

"Do it at two," Inez said. "Or she goes someplace where they will do it at two."

"Move the patient, you could confuse the cause of death." The resident looked at the detectives for corroboration. "Cloud it. Legally."

"I don't give a fuck about the cause of death," Inez said.

There was a silence.

"I'd say do it at two," the older of the two homicide detectives said.

"I notice you're still getting what you want," Jack Lovett said to Inez.

They did it at two and again at ten in the morning and each time it was flat but the chief neurologist, after consultation with the homicide detectives and the hospital lawyers, said that a fourth flat reading would make everyone more comfortable. A fourth flat reading would guarantee that removal of support could not be argued as cause of death. A fourth flat reading would be something everyone could live with.

"Everybody except Janet," Inez said, but she said it only to Jack Lovett.

Eight hours later they did it again and again it was flat and at 7:40 P.M. on Thursday, March 27, Janet Christian Ziegler was pronounced dead. During most of the almost twenty-four hours preceding this pronouncement Inez had waited on a large sofa in an empty surgical waiting room. During much of this time Jack Lovett was with her. Of whatever Jack Lovett said to Inez during those almost twenty-four hours she could distinctly remember later only a story he told her about a woman who cooked for him in Saigon in 1970. This woman had tried, over a period of some months, to poison selected dinner guests with oleander leaves. She had minced the leaves into certain soup bowls, very fine, a chiffonade of hemotoxins. Although none of these guests died at least two, a Reuters correspondent and an AID analyst, fell ill, but the cook was not suspected until her son-in-law, who believed himself cuckolded by the woman's daughter, came to Jack Lovett with the story.

"What was the point," Inez said.

"Whose point?"

"The cook's." Inez was drinking a bottle of beer that Jack Lovett had brought to the hospital. "What was the cook's motive?"

"Her motive." Jack Lovett seemed not interested in

169

this part of the story. "Turned out she was just deluded. A strictly personal deal. Disappointing, actually. At first I thought I was onto something."

Inez had finished the beer and studied Jack Lovett's face. She considered asking him what he had thought he was onto but decided against it. After this little incident with the cook he had given up on housekeeping, he said. After this little incident with the cook he had gone back to staying at the Duc. Whenever he had to be in Saigon.

"You liked it there," Inez said. The beer had relaxed her and she was beginning to fall asleep, holding Jack Lovett's hand. "You loved it. Didn't you."

"Some days were better than others, I guess." Jack Lovett let go of Inez's hand and laid his jacket over her bare legs. "Oh sure," he said then. "It was kind of the place to be."

Occasionally during that night and day Dick Ziegler came to the hospital, but on the whole he seemed relieved to leave the details of the watch to Inez. "Janet doesn't even know we're here," Dick Ziegler said each time he came to the hospital.

"I'm not here for Janet," Inez said finally, but Dick Ziegler ignored her.

"Doesn't even know we're here," he repeated.

Quite often during that night and day Billy Dillon came to the hospital. "Naturally you're overwrought," Billy Dillon said each time he came to the hospital. "Which is why I'm not taking this seriously. Ask me what I think about what Inez is doing, I'd say no comment. She's overwrought."

"Listen," Billy Dillon said the last time he came to the hospital. "We're picking up incoming on the King Crab flank. Harry takes the Warner's plane to Seattle to pick up Jessie for the funeral, Jessie informs Harry she doesn't go to funerals."

Inez had looked at Billy Dillon.

"Well?" Billy Dillon said.

"Well what?"

"What should I tell Harry?"

"Tell him he should have advanced it better," Inez Victor said.

13

I SHOULD tell you something about Jessie
Victor that very few people understood. Harry Victor for example never understood it. Inez understood
it only dimly. Here it is: Jessie never thought of herself as a problem. She never considered her use of
heroin an act of rebellion, or a way of life, or even a
bad habit of particular remark; she considered it a
consumer decision. Jessie Victor used heroin simply
because she preferred heroin to coffee, aspirin, and
cigarettes, as well as to movies, records, cosmetics,
clothes, and lunch. She had been subjected repeatedly
to the usual tests, and each battery showed her to be
anxious, highly motivated, more intelligent than Adlai, and not given to falsification. Perhaps because she
lacked the bent for falsification she did not have a
notable sense of humor. What she did have was a certain incandescent inscrutability, a kind of luminous
gravity, and it was always startling to hear her dismiss
someone, in that grave low voice that thrilled Inez as
sharply when Jessie was eighteen as it had when Jessie
was two, as "an asshole." "You asshole" was what
Jessie called Adlai, the night he and Harry Victor arrived in Seattle to pick her up for Janet's funeral and
Jessie declined to go. Jessie did agree to have dinner

with them, while the Warner Communications G-2 was being refueled, but dinner had gone badly.

"The crux of it is finding a way to transfer anti-war sentiment to a multiple-issue program," Adlai had said at dinner. He was telling Harry Victor about an article he proposed to write for the op-ed page of the New York *Times*. "It's something we've been tossing back and forth in Cambridge."

"Interesting," Harry Victor said. "Let me vet it. What do you think, Jess?"

"I think he shouldn't say 'Cambridge,' " Jessie said.

"Possibly you were nodding out when I went up there," Adlai said, "but Cambridge happens to be where I go to school."

"Maybe so," Jessie said, "but you don't happen to go to Harvard."

"OK, guys. You both fouled." Harry Victor turned to Adlai. "I could sound somebody out at the *Times*. If you're serious."

"I'm serious. It's time. Bring my generation into the dialogue, if you see my point."

"You asshole," Jessie said.

"Well," Harry Victor said after Adlai had left the table. "How are things otherwise?"

"I'm ready to leave."

"You said you weren't going. You have a principle. You don't go to funerals. This is a new principle on me, but never mind, you made your case. I accept it. As a principle."

"I don't mean leave for Janet's funeral. I mean actually leave. Period. This place. Seattle."

"You haven't finished the program."

"The program," Jessie said, "is for assholes."

"Just a minute," Harry said.

"I did the detox, I'm clean, I don't see the point."

"What do you mean you did the detox, the game plan here wasn't detox, it was methadone."

"I don't like methadone."

"Why not?"

"Because," Jessie had said patiently, "it doesn't make me feel good."

"It makes you feel bad?"

"It doesn't make me feel bad, no." Jessie had given this question her full attention. "It just doesn't make me feel good."

There had been a silence.

"What is it you want to do exactly?" Harry had said then.

"I want—" Jessie was studying a piece of bread that she seemed to have rolled into a ball. "To get on with my regular life. Make some headway, you know?"

"That's fine. Good news. Admirable."

"Get into my career."

"Which is what exactly?"

Jessie was breaking the ball of bread into little pellets.

"Don't misread me, Jessie. This is all admirable. My only point is that you need a program." Harry Victor found himself warming to the idea of the projected program. "A plan. Two plans, actually. Which dovetail. A long-range plan and a short-term plan. What's your long-range plan?"

"I'm not running for Congress," Jessie said. "If that's what you mean."

There seemed to Harry so plaintive a note in this that he let it go. "Well then. All right. How about your immediate plan?"

Jessie picked up another piece of bread.

Something in Harry Victor snapped. He had been trying for the past hour to avoid any contemplation of why Inez had walked out of Dwight Christian's house the night before with Jack Lovett. Billy Dillon had told him. "You have to think she's overwrought," Billy Dillon had said. "I have to think she's got loony timing," Harry Victor had said. Early on in this dinner he had tried out the overwrought angle on Jessie and Adlai. "I wouldn't be surprised if your mother were a little overwrought," he had said. Adlai had put down the menu and said that he wanted a shrimp cocktail and the New York stripper, medium bloody, sour cream and chives on the spud. Jessie had put down the menu and stared at him, he imagined fishily, from under the straw tennis visor she had worn to dinner.

Jessie had stared at him fishily from under her tennis visor and Adlai had wanted the New York stripper medium bloody and Inez had walked out of Dwight Christian's house with Jack Lovett and now Jessie was tearing her bread into little chicken-shit pellets.

"Could you do me a favor? Jessie? Could you either eat the bread or leave it alone?"

Jessie had put her hands in her lap.

"I'm still kind of working on the immediate plan part," she said after a while. "Actually."

In fact Jessie Victor did have an immediate plan that Thursday evening in Seattle, the same plan she had mentioned in its less immediate form to Inez at Christmas, the plan Inez had selectively neglected to mention when she described her visit with Jessie to Harry and Adlai: the plan, if the convergence of yearning and rumor and isolation on which Jessie was operating in Seattle could be called a plan, to get a job in Vietnam.

Inez had not mentioned this plan to Harry because she did not believe it within the range of the possible.

Jessie did not mention this plan to Harry because she did not believe it to be the kind of plan that Harry would understand.

I see Jessie's point of view here. Harry would have talked specifics. Harry would have asked Jessie if she had read a newspaper lately. Harry would not have understood that specifics made no difference to Jessie. Getting a job in Vietnam seemed to Jessie a first step that had actually presented itself, a chance to put herself at last in opportunity's way, and because she believed that whatever went on there was only politics and that politics was for assholes she would have remained undeflected, that March night in 1975, the same night as it happened that the American evacuation of Da Nang deteriorated into uncontrolled rioting, by anything she might have heard or seen or read in a newspaper.

If in fact Jessie ever read a newspaper.

Which seemed to both Inez and Harry Victor a doubtful proposition.

When word reached them in Honolulu on the following Sunday night, Easter Sunday night 1975, the night before Janet's funeral, that three hours after the Warner Communications G-2 left Seattle, bringing Harry and Adlai Victor down to Honolulu, Jessie had walked out of the clinic that specialized in the treatment of adolescent chemical dependency and talked her way onto a C-5A transport that landed seventeen-and-one-half hours later (refueling twice in flight) at Tan Son Nhut, Saigon. "Maybe she heard she could score there," Adlai said, and Inez slapped him.

14

S H E did it with no passport (her passport was in her otherwise empty stash box in the apartment on Central Park West) and a joke press card that somebody from *Life* had made up for her during the 1972 campaign. This press card had failed to get Jessie Victor at age fifteen into the backstage area at Nassau Coliseum during a Pink Floyd concert but it got her at age eighteen onto the C-5A to Saigon. This seems astonishing now, but we forget how confused and febrile those few weeks in 1975 actually were, the "reassessments" and the "calculated gambles" and the infusions of supplemental aid giving way even as they were reported to the lurid phantasmagoria of air lifts and marines on the roof and stranded personnel and tarmacs littered with shoes and broken toys. In the immediate glamour of the revealed crisis many things happened that could not have happened a few months earlier or a few weeks later, and what happened to Jessie Victor was one of them. Clearly an American girl who landed at Tan Son Nhut should have been detained there, but Jessie Victor was not. Clearly an American girl who landed at Tan Son Nhut with no passport should not have been stamped through immigration on the basis of a New York driver's license, but Jessie Victor was. Clearly an American girl with no passport, a New York driver's license and a straw tennis visor should not have been able to walk out of the littered makeshift terminal at Tan Son Nhut and, observed by several people who did nothing to stop her, get on a bus to Cholon, but Jessie Victor had done just that. Or so it appeared.

By the time Jack Lovett arrived at the house on Manoa Road that Easter Sunday night with the story about the American girl who appeared to be Jessie, the blond American girl who had left a New York driver's license at Tan Son Nhut in lieu of a visa, Inez and Harry Victor were speaking to each other only in the presence of other people.

They had been civil at the required meals but avoided the optional.

They had slept in the same room but not the same bed.

"You're overwrought," Harry had said on Friday night. "You're under a strain."

"Actually I'm not in the least overwrought," Inez had said. "I'm sad. Sad is different from overwrought."

"Why not just have another drink," Harry had said. "For a change."

By Saturday morning the argument was smoldering one more time on the remote steppes of the 1972 campaign. By Saturday evening it had jumped the break and was burning uncontained. "Do you know what I particularly couldn't stand," Inez had said. "I particularly couldn't stand it at Miami when you said you were the voice of a generation that had taken fire on the battlefields of Vietnam and Chicago."

"I'm amazed you were sober enough to notice. At Miami."

"I'd drop that theme if I were you. I think you've gotten about all the mileage you're going to get out of that."

"Out of what?"

"Harry Victor's Burden. I was sober enough to notice you didn't start speaking for this generation until after the second caucus. You were only the voice of a generation that had taken fire on the battlefields of Vietnam and Chicago after you knew you didn't have the numbers. In addition to which. Moreover. Actually that was never your generation. Actually you were older."

There had been a silence.

"Let me take a leap forward here," Harry had said. "Speaking of 'older.' "

Inez had waited.

"I don't think you chose a particularly appropriate way to observe your sister's death. Maybe I'm wrong."

Inez had looked out the window for a long time before she spoke. "Add it up, you and I didn't have such a bad time," she said finally. "Net."

"I'm supposed to notice the past tense. Is that it?"

Inez did not turn from the window. It was dark. She had lived in the north so long that she always forgot how fast the light went. She had gone late that afternoon to pick up the dress in which Dick Ziegler wanted Janet buried and the light had gone while she was still on Janet's beach. "You pick a dress," Dick Ziegler had said. "You go. I can't look in her closet." After Inez found a dress she had sat on Janet's bed and called Jack Lovett on Janet's antique telephone. Jack Lovett had told her to wait on Janet's beach. "Listen," Inez had said when she saw him. "That pink dress she wore in Jakarta is in her closet. She has four-teen pink dresses. I counted them. Fourteen." She had been talking through tears. "Fourteen pink dresses all hanging next to each other. Didn't anybody ever tell her? She didn't look good in pink?" There on the beach with Jack Lovett in the last light of the day Inez had cried for the first time that week, but back in the house on Manoa Road with Harry she had felt herself sealed off again, her damage control mechanism still intact.

"I think I deserve a little better than a change of tense," Harry said.

"Don't dramatize," Inez said.

Or she did not.

She had either said "Don't dramatize" to Harry that Saturday evening or she had said "I love him" to Harry that Saturday evening. It seemed more likely that she had said "Don't dramatize" but she had wanted to say "I love him" and she did not remember which. She did remember that the actual words "Jack Lovett" remained unsaid by either of them until Sun-day night.

"Your friend Lovett's downstairs," Harry had said then.

"Jack," Inez said, but Harry had left the room.

Jack Lovett repeated the details of the story about the American girl at Tan Son Nhut twice, once for Inez and Harry and Billy Dillon and again when Dwight Christian and Adlai came in. The details sounded even less probable in the second telling. The C-5A, the press card. The tennis visor. The bus to Cholon.

"I see," Harry kept saying. "Yes."

Jack Lovett had first heard Jessie's name that Sunday morning from one of the people to whom he regularly talked on the flight line at Tan Son Nhut. It had taken five further calls and the rest of the day to locate the New York driver's license that had been left at immigration in lieu of a visa.

"I see," Harry said. "Yes. Then you haven't actually seen this license."

"How could I have seen the license, Harry? The license is in Saigon."

Inez watched Jack Lovett unfold an envelope covered with scratched notes. Lovett. Jack. Your friend Lovett.

"Jessica Christian Victor?" Jack Lovett was squinting at his notes. "Born February 23, 1957?"

Harry did not look at Inez.

"Hair blond, eyes gray? Height five-four? Weight one-hundred-ten?" Jack Lovett folded the envelope and put it in his coat pocket. "The address was yours."

"But you didn't write it down."

Jack Lovett looked at Harry. "Because I knew it, Harry. 135 Central Park West."

There was a silence.

"Her weight was up when she got her license," Inez said finally. "She only weighs a hundred and three."

"The fact that somebody had Jessie's license doesn't necessarily mean it was Jessie," Harry said.

"Not necessarily," Jack Lovett said. "No."

"I mean Jesus Christ," Harry said. "Every kid in the country's got a tennis visor."

"What about a tennis visor?" Inez said.

"She was wearing one," Adlai said. "At dinner. In Seattle."

"Never mind the fucking tennis visor." Harry picked up the telephone. "You got the Seattle number, Billy?"

Billy Dillon took a small flat leather notebook from his pocket and opened it.

"I have it," Inez said.

"So does Billy." Harry drummed his fingers on the table as Billy Dillon dialed. "This is Harry Victor," he said after a moment. "I'd like to speak to Jessie."

Inez looked at Jack Lovett.

Jack Lovett was studying his envelope again.

"I see," Harry said. "Yes. Of course."

"Shit," Billy Dillon said.

"There's a kid who flew in this morning from Tan Son Nhut," Jack Lovett said. "A radar specialist who's been working Air America Operations."

"Her aunt, yes," Harry said. "No, I have it. Thank you." He replaced the receiver. He still did not look at Inez. "Your move," he said after a while.

"This kid is supposed to have seen her," Jack Lovett said.

"Did he or didn't he?" Harry said.

"I don't know, Harry." Jack Lovett's voice was even. "I haven't talked to him yet."

"Then it's not relevant," Harry said.

"She only weighs a hundred and three," Inez repeated.

"That's the second time you've said that," Harry said. "It's about as relevant as this radar specialist of Lovett's. It doesn't mean anything."

"I'll tell you what it means," Dwight Christian said. "It means she'll fit right in."

Harry stared at Dwight Christian, then looked at Billy Dillon.

"Welcome to hard times, pal," Billy Dillon said. "Try mentioning Sea Meadow."

"In fact she'll outweigh nine-tenths of them," Dwight Christian said. "Nine-tenths of the citizenry of Saigon."

"I knew you could dress that up." Billy Dillon looked at Harry. "You want to make a pass through State? Usual channels?"

"Usual channels, Mickey Mouse," Dwight Christian said. "Call the White House. Get them to light a fire under the embassy. Lay on some pressure. Demand her release."

"Her release from what?" Harry said.

"From the citizenry of Saigon," Billy Dillon said. "Follow the ball."

There was a silence.

"I may not phrase things as elegantly as you two, but I do know what I want." Dwight Christian's voice had turned hard and measured. "I want her out of there. Harry?"

"It's not quite that simple, Dwight."

"Not if you're from Washington," Dwight Christian said. "I suppose not. Since I'm not from Washington, I don't quite see what the problem is."

"Dwight," Inez said. "The problem—"

"I had a foreman taken hostage on the Iguassú Falls project, I didn't phrase things so elegantly there, either, not being from Washington, but I goddamn well got him out."

"—The problem, Dwight, is that nobody took Jessie hostage."

Dwight Christian looked at Inez.

"She just went," Inez said.

"I know that, sweetheart." The hardness had gone out of Dwight Christian's voice. "I just want somebody to tell me why."

Which was when Adlai said maybe she heard she could score there.

Which was when Inez slapped Adlai.

Which was when Harry said keep your hands off my son.

185

But Dad, Adlai kept saying in the silence that followed. But Dad. Mom.

Aloha oe.

Billy Dillon once asked me if I thought Inez would have left that night had Jack Lovett not been there. Since human behavior seems to me essentially circumstantial I have not much feeling for this kind of question. The answer of course is no, but the answer is irrelevant, because Jack Lovett was there.

Jack Lovett was one of the circumstances that night.

Jack Lovett was there and Jessie was in Saigon, another of the circumstances that night.

Jessie was in Saigon and the radar specialist who was said to have seen her was to meet Jack Lovett at the Playboy Arcade in Waianae. This radar specialist who had or had not seen Jessie was meeting Jack Lovett in Waianae and an electrician who had worked on the installation of the research reactor at Dalat was meeting Jack Lovett in Wahiawa.

The research reactor at Dalat was a circumstance that night only in that it happened to be a card Jack Lovett was dealing that spring.

Jack Lovett did not see any immediate way to get the fuel out but he wanted to know, for future calculation, how much of this fuel was being left, in what condition, and for whom.

The research reactor at Dalat was a thread Jack Lovett had not yet tied in his attempt to transfer the phantom business predicated on the perpetuation of the assistance effort, which was why, on that Easter Sunday night in 1975, he took Inez first to meet the radar specialist at the Playboy Arcade in Waianae and then across Kolekole Pass to meet the electrician at the Happy Talk Lounge in Wahiawa.

The off-limits Happy Talk in Wahiawa.

The Happy Talk in Wahiawa across the bridge from Schofield Barracks.

Where Inez stood with her back against the juke-box and her arms around Jack Lovett.

Where The Mamas and the Papas sang "Dream a Little Dream of Me."

The radar specialist had been on the nod.

"I don't need the hassle," the radar specialist had said.

The electrician had already left the Happy Talk but had left a note with the bartender.

Da Nang going, that dude at Dalat definitely a wipe-out, the note read.

On the screen above the bar there were the helicopters. There were the helicopters lifting off the roof of the American mission and there were the helicopters vanishing into the fireball above the ammo dump and there were the helicopters ditching in the oil slick off the *Pioneer Contender*.

"Fucking Arvin finally shooting each other," the bartender said.

"Oh shit, Inez," Jack Lovett said. "Harry Victor's wife."

"Listen," Inez said. "It's too late for the correct thing. Forget the correct thing."

Which is how Jack Lovett and Inez Victor happened that Easter Sunday night in 1975 to take the Singapore Airlines flight that leaves Honolulu at 3:45 A.M. and at 9:40 A.M. one day later lands at Kai Tak, Hong Kong.

Recently when I took this flight I thought of Inez, who described it as an eleven-hour dawn.

Inez said she never closed her eyes.

Inez said she could still feel the cold of the window against her cheek.

Inez said the 3:45 A.M. flight from Honolulu to Hong Kong was exactly the way she hoped dying would be.

Dawn all the way.

Something to see, as Jack Lovett had said at the Happy Talk about another dawn in another year. Something to behold.

It occurs to me that Inez Victor's behavior the night she flew to Hong Kong may not have been so circumstantial after all.

She had to have a passport with her, didn't she?

What does that suggest?

You tell me.

THREE

1

___

THE day Jack Lovett flew down to Saigon the rain began in Hong Kong. The rain muddied the streets, stiffened the one pair of shoes Inez had with her, broke the blossoms from the bauhinia tree on the balcony of the apartment in which Jack Lovett had told her to wait and obscured the view of the Happy Valley track from the bedroom window. The rain reminded her of Honolulu. The rain and the obscured horizon and the breaking of the blossoms and the persistent smell of mildew in the small apartment all reminded her of Honolulu but it was colder in Hong Kong. She was always cold. Every morning after Jack Lovett left Inez would wake early in the slight chill and put on the galoshes and macintosh she had found in the otherwise empty closet and set out to walk. She developed a route. She would walk down Queen's Road and over behind the Anglican cathedral and up Garden Road to the American consulate, where she would sit in the reception room and read newspapers.

Quite often in the reception room of the American consulate on Garden Road Inez read about Harry Victor's relatives. In the *South China Morning Post* she read that Harry Victor's wife had not been present at the funeral of Harry Victor's sister-in-law, a private service in Honolulu after which Senator Victor declined to speak to reporters. In the Asian edition of the *International Herald-Tribune* she read that Harry Victor's father-in-law had required treatment at the Honolulu City and County Jail for superficial wounds inflicted during an apparent suicide attempt with a Bic razor. In the international editions of both *Time* and *Newsweek* she read that Harry Victor's daughter was ironically or mysteriously missing in Vietnam.

"Ironically" was the word used by *Time*, and "mysteriously" by *Newsweek*. Both *Time* and *Newsweek* used "missing," as did the *South China Morning Post*, the Asian editions of both the *Wall Street Journal* and the *International Herald-Tribune*, the *Straits Times*, and the pouched copies of the New York *Times* and the Washington *Post* that arrived at the consulate three days after publication. "Missing" did not seem to Inez to quite cover it. The pilots of downed fighters were said to be "missing," and correspondents last seen in ambush situations. "Missing" suggested some line of duty that did not quite encompass getting on a C-5A transport in Seattle and flying to Saigon to look for a job. Possibly that was the ironic part, or even the mysterious.

By the time Inez finished reading the papers it would be close to noon, and she would walk from the consulate on up Garden Road to what seemed to be a Chinese nursery school, with a terrace roofed in corrugated plastic under which the children played. She would stand in the rain and watch the children until, at the ping of a little bell, they formed a line and marched inside, and then she would take a taxi back to the apartment and hang the macintosh on the shower door to dry and set the galoshes behind the door. She had no idea to whom the galoshes and macintosh belonged. She had no idea to whom the apartment belonged.

"Somebody in Vientiane," Jack Lovett had said when she asked.

She presumed it was a woman because the galoshes and macintosh were small. She presumed the woman was an American because the only object in the medicine cabinet, a plastic bottle of aspirin tablets, was the house brand of a drugstore she knew to be in New York. She presumed that the American woman was a reporter because there was a standard Smith-Corona typewriter and a copy of *Modern English Usage* on the kitchen table, and a paperback copy of *Homage to Catalonia* in the drawer of the bed table. In Inez's experience all reporters had paperback copies of *Homage to Catalonia*, and kept them in the same place where they kept the matches and the candle and the notebook, for when the hotel was bombed. When she asked Jack Lovett if the person in Vientiane to whom the apartment belonged was in fact an American woman reporter he had shrugged.

"It doesn't matter," he said. "It's fine."

After that when Inez read the newspapers in the reception room of the American consulate she made a

193

point of noticing the byline on any story originating in Vientiane, looking for a woman's name, but never found one.

The telephone in this apartment never rang. Jack Lovett got his messages in Hong Kong at a small hotel off Connaught Road, and it was this number that Inez had given Adlai when she reached him in Honolulu the day she arrived. Because Harry had hung up mid-sentence when she called him from Wahiawa to say she was going to Hong Kong she made this call person-to-person to Adlai, but Harry had come on the line first.

"I happen to know you're in Hong Kong," Harry had said.

"Of course you happen to know I'm in Hong Kong," Inez had said. "I told you I was going."

"Will you speak to this party," the operator had kept saying. "Is this your party?"

"You hung up," Inez had said.

"No," Harry had said. "This is not her party."

"This doesn't have anything to do with you," Inez had said when Adlai finally picked up. "I just wanted to make sure you knew that."

"Dad told me." Adlai had made this sound slightly prosecutorial. "What does it have to do with?"

"Just not with you."

"What am I supposed to tell Dad?"

Inez had considered this. "Tell him hello," she said finally.

That had been Tuesday in Hong Kong and Monday in Honolulu.

It had been Wednesday the second of April in Hong Kong when Jack Lovett flew down to Saigon to look for Jessie.

Twice during that first week, the week of the rain, he had come back up to Hong Kong unexpectedly, once on an Air America transport with eighty-three third-country nationals who had been identified with American interests and once on a chartered Pan American 707 with the officers and cash reserves of the Saigon branches of the Bank of America, the First National City Bank, and the Chase Manhattan. The first time he came up it had been for only a few hours, which he spent placing calls from the telephone in the apartment, but the second time he had spent the night, and they had driven out to the Repulse Bay and taken a room overlooking the sea. They had ordered dinner in the room and slept and woke and slept again and whenever they were awake Jack Lovett had talked. He had seemed to regard the room at the Repulse Bay as neutral ground on which he could talk as he had not talked in the apartment that belonged to somebody in Vientiane. He talked all night. He talked to Inez but as if to himself. Certain words and phrases kept recurring.

Fixed-wing phase.

Tiger Ops.

Black flights.

Extraction.

Assets.

AID was without assets.

USIA was without assets.

By assets Jack Lovett had seemed to mean aircraft, aircraft and money. The Defense Attaché Office had assets. It was increasingly imperative to develop your own assets because without private assets no one could guarantee extraction. No one could guarantee extraction because they were living in a dream world down there. Amateur hour down there. Pencil pushers down there.

Each time Jack Lovett said "down there" he would glance toward the windows that opened on the water, as if "down there" were visible, nine hundred miles of South China Sea telescoped by the pressure of his obsession. Toward dawn he was talking about the lists they were making down there. They had finally decided to make a count of priority evacuees in case extraction was necessary.

In case.

Inez should note "in case."

"In case" was proof the inmates were running the bin.

Because the various agencies had been unable to agree on the count each agency was drawing up its own list. Some people said the lists would add up to a hundred-fifty-thousand priority evacuees, others said ten times that number. Nobody seemed in any rush to make it definite. They were talking about evacuating twenty years of American contacts, not to mention their own fat American asses, but they were still talking as if they had another twenty years to do it. Twenty years and the applause of the local population. An inter-agency task force had been appointed.

To shake this down. The task force had met for dinner at the residence, met for goddamn dinner at the goddamn residence, add a little more lard to those asses, and by the time the cigars were passed they did not yet know whether they had a hundred-fifty-thousand priority evacuees or ten times that number but they did know what they needed.

They needed a wall map.

They needed a wall map of what they kept calling Metro Saigon.

This wall map had been requisitioned.

Through General Services.

They were getting their wall map any day now, and what they would do when they got it was this: they would make a population density plot. In other words they would plot, with little colored pins, the locations of a few types of people they might want to invite to the final extraction.

In case.

Strictly in case.

"Types" of people, right.

A little green pin for every holder of an embassy ration card.

A little yellow pin for every holder of a DAO liquor ration card.

A little red pin for every current member of the Cercle Sportif. Note "current." Behind on the dues, forget it.

The little white pins were the real stroke. Follow this. There was going to be an analysis of all taxi dispatch records for the period between the first of January and the first of April. Then there would be a little white pin placed on the map showing every location in Metro Saigon to which a taxi had been dispatched. Too bad for the guys who drove their own cars. Around Metro Saigon. Taken a cab, they'd be on the map. This map was going to be a genuine work of art. Anybody down there had any feeling for posterity, they'd get this map out and put it under glass at the State Department.

Pins intact.

Memento mori Metro Saigon.

By the time he stopped talking the room was light.

Inez sat on the edge of the bed and began brushing her hair.

"So what do you think," Jack Lovett said.

"I don't know."

Through the half-closed shutters Inez could see the early light on the water. It occurred to her for the first time that this was the same sea she had looked on with Jessie, the day there had been no baby cobras in the borrowed garden and Harry had been at the situation briefing in Saigon. Now there was about to be no more situation and Jessie was in Saigon and Jack Lovett was going back down to Saigon but Jack Lovett might not find her before it happened.

Nobody even knew what "it" was.

That was what he was telling her.

She brushed her hair harder. "I don't know how an evacuation is run."

"Not this way."

"She's not on anybody's list, is she." Inez found that she could not say Jessie's name. "She's not on the map."

Jack Lovett got up and opened the shutters wide. For a while the rain had stopped but now it was falling hard again, falling through the patchy sunlight, glistening on the palms outside the window and flooding the broken fountain in front of the hotel.

"Not unless she happened to join the Cercle Sportif," Jack Lovett said. "No." He closed the shutters again and turned back toward Inez. "Put down the hairbrush and look at me," he said. "Do you think I'd leave her there?"

"You might not find her."

"I always found you," Jack Lovett said. "I guess I can find your daughter."

2

In fact Jack Lovett did find Inez Victor's daughter.

In fact Jack Lovett found Inez Victor's daughter that very day, found her by what he called dumb luck, just got on the regular Air Vietnam flight from Hong Kong to Saigon and landed at Tan Son Nhut and half an hour later he was looking at Jessie Victor.

Jack Lovett called this dumb luck but you or I might not have had the same dumb luck.

You or I for example might not have struck up the connection with the helicopter maintenance instructor who happened to be one of the other two passengers on the Air Vietnam 707 to Saigon that day.

Jack Lovett did.

Jack Lovett struck up a connection with this helicopter maintenance instructor the same way he had struck up connections with all those embassy drivers and oil riggers and airline stewardesses and assistant professors of English literature traveling on Fulbright fellowships and tropical agronomists traveling under the auspices of the Rockefeller Foundation and desk clerks and ticket agents and salesmen of rice converters and coco dryers and Dutch pesticides and German pharmaceuticals.

By reflex.

The helicopter maintenance instructor who happened to be one of the two other passengers on the Air Vietnam 707 that day had last been in Saigon in 1973, when his contract was terminated. He had been in Los Angeles working for Hughes but now he was coming back to look for the wife and little girl he had left in 1973. The wife had been with her family in Pleiku and he had gotten a call from her saying that the little girl had been blinded on a C-130 during the evacuation south when a leaking hydraulic line overhead sprayed liquid into her face. The wife said Saigon was still safe but he thought it was time to come find her. He had the address she had given him but according to a buddy he had contacted this address did not check out. The helicopter maintenance instructor had seemed cheerful at the beginning of the flight but after two Seagram Sevens his mood had darkened.

What had she done to get on the C-130 in the first place?

Didn't everybody else walk out of Pleiku?

What about the fucking address?

Jack Lovett had offered him a ride into Saigon and the helicopter maintenance instructor had wanted to make one stop, to check the address with a bartender he used to know at the Legion club.

Which was where Jack Lovett found Jessie Victor. Serving drinks and French fries at the American

Legion club on the main road between Tan Son Nhut and Saigon.

Still wearing her tennis visor.

An *ao dai* and her tennis visor.

"Hey, no sweat, I'm staying," Jessie had said to Jack Lovett when he told her to sign off her shift and get in the car. "This dude who comes in has a friend at the embassy, he'll get the word when they pull the plug."

Jessie had insisted she was staying but Jack Lovett had said a few words to the bartender.

The words Jack Lovett said were Harry goddamn Victor's daughter.

"You know this plug you were talking about," Jack Lovett said then to Jessie. "I just pulled it."

3

"Y ou're looking for a guy in the wood-work, the Legion club is where you'd look," Jack Lovett said when he finally got through to Inez in Hong Kong. "Christ almighty. The Legion club. I covered Mimi's, I don't know how I missed the Legion club."

He was calling from the Duc.

He had left Jessie for the night at the apartment of a woman he referred to only as "B.J.," an intelligence analyst at the Defense Attaché Office.

B.J. would put Jessie up until he could get her out.

B.J. would take fine care of Jessie.

B.J. was even that night sounding out the air lift supervisor at Tiger Ops about the possibility of placing Jessie on a flight to Travis as an orphan escort. These orphans all had escorts, sure they did, that was the trick, the trick was to melt out as many nonessentials as possible without calling it an evacuation. They might or might not be orphans, these orphans, but they sure as hell had escorts. The whole goddamn DAO was trying to melt out with the orphans.

Which was what they didn't know at the Legion club.

Which was where you looked if you were looking for a guy in the woodwork.

"About these flights to Travis," Inez said.

"Looking, hell, look no further." Jack Lovett could not seem to get over the obviousness of finding Jessie at the Legion club. "This is it. This is the woodwork. American Legion Post No. 34. Through These Portals Pass America's Proudest Fighting Men, it says over the door to the can. Through those portals pass every AWOL and contract cowboy in Southeast Asia. Guys who came over with the Air Cav in '66. Guys who evacuated China in '49. Dudes. Dudes who think they've got a friend at the embassy."

"That was an orphan flight to Travis that crashed," Inez said. The connection was going and she had trouble hearing him. "Last week."

"There are other options," Jack Lovett said.

"Other options to crashing?"

"Other flights, Inez. Other kinds of flights. She's fine with B.J., there's no immediate problem. I'll check it out. I'll get her on a good flight."

Inez said nothing.

"Inez," Jack Lovett said. "This kid of yours is one of the world's great survivors. I take her kicking and screaming to B.J.'s, half an hour later they're splitting a bucket of Kentucky fried and comparing eye makeup. The lights go off, Jessie tells B.J. she knows where they could liberate a Signal Corps generator. 'Liberate' is what she says. She got here any earlier, she'd be running the rackets."

Inez said nothing. The connection was now crossed with another call, and she could hear laughter, and sharp bursts of Cantonese.

"She's as tough as you are," Jack Lovett said.

"That never stopped any plane from crashing," Inez said just before the line went to dial tone.

After Inez hung up she tried to call Harry at the apartment on Central Park West. Harry's private line rang busy and when she tried one of the other numbers Billy Dillon answered.

"This is pretty funny," Billy Dillon said when she told him about Jessie. "This is actually funny as hell."

"What's actually funny about it?"

"I don't know, Inez. You don't find it funny we're sending bar girls to Saigon, I can't help you. Hey. Inez. Do us all a favor? Tell Harry yourself?"

Inez had told Harry herself.

"I see," Harry said. "Yes."

There had been a silence.

"So," Inez said. "There it is."

"Serving drinks. Yes. I'll get hold of Adlai at school."

"What's he doing at school?"

"What do you mean, 'what's he doing at school'? You think Adlai should be serving drinks too?"

"I mean I thought he was doing this internship with you. I thought he didn't have to be back until May."

"He wanted to organize something," Harry said. "But that's not the point."

"Organize what?"

"Some kind of event."

"What kind of event?"

Harry had hesitated. "A vigil for the liberation of Saigon," he said finally.

Inez had said nothing.

"He's eighteen years old, Inez." Harry had sounded defensive. "He wanted to make a statement."

"I didn't say anything."

"Very eloquent. Your silence."

Inez said nothing.

"Jessie's tramping around Saigon, you're off with your war-lover, Adlai tries to make a statement and you've got nothing to say."

"I'm going to pretend you didn't say that."

"Fine then," Harry said. "Pretend what you want."

All that night Inez lay awake in the apartment that belonged to somebody in Vientiane and listened to the short-wave radio that Jack Lovett had left there. On the short-wave radio she could get Saigon and Bangkok. Jack Lovett had told her what to listen for. Jack Lovett had also told her that it was too soon to hear what he had told her to listen for but she listened anyway, whenever she could not sleep or wanted to hear a human voice.

"Mother wants you to call home," the American Service Radio announcer in Saigon would say when it was time for the final phase of the evacuation, and then a certain record would be played.

The record to be played was Bing Crosby singing "I'm Dreaming of a White Christmas."

"I could do better than that," Inez had said when

Jack Lovett told her what to listen for. "I mean in the middle of April. Out of the blue in the middle of April. I could do considerably better than 'Mother wants you to call home' and 'I'm Dreaming of a White Christmas.' "

"What's your point," Jack Lovett said.

"It's not just the best secret signal I ever heard about."

"It's not going to be just the best evacuation you ever heard about either," Jack Lovett had said. "You want to get down to fine strokes."

Toward four in the morning Inez got up from the bed and sat by the window and smoked a cigarette in the dark. The window was open and rain splashed on the balcony outside. Because it was still too soon to hear the American Service Radio announcer in Saigon say "Mother wants you to call home" Inez moved the dial back and forth and finally got what seemed to be a BBC correspondent interviewing former officials of the government of the Republic of Vietnam who had just been flown to Nakhon Phanom in Thailand.

"No more hopes from the American side," one of them said.

"The Americans would not come back again," another said. "*En un mot* bye-bye."

Their voices were pleasant and formal.

The transmission faded in and out.

As she listened to the rain and to the voices fading in and out from Nakhon Phanom Inez thought about Harry in New York and Adlai at school and Jessie at B.J.'s and it occurred to her that for the first time in almost twenty years she was not particularly interested in any of them.

Responsible for them in a limited way, yes, but not interested in them.

They were definitely connected to her but she could no longer grasp her own or their uniqueness, her own or their difference, genius, special claim. What difference did it make in the long run what she thought, or Harry thought, or Jessie or Adlai did? What difference did it make in the long run whether any one person got the word, called home, dreamed of a white Christmas? The world that night was full of people flying from place to place and fading in and out and there was no reason why she or Harry or Jessie or Adlai, or for that matter Jack Lovett or B.J. or the woman in Vientiane on whose balcony the rain now fell, should be exempted from the general movement.

Just because they believed they had a home to call.

Just because they were Americans.

No.

En un mot bye-bye.

FOUR

1

I see now that the state of rather eerie serenity in which I found Inez Victor in Kuala Lumpur had its genesis eight months before, during this period in Hong Kong when it came to her attention that her passport did not excuse her from what she characterized to me as "the long view." By "the long view" I believe she meant history, or more exactly the particular undertow of having and not having, the convulsions of a world largely unaffected by the individual efforts of anyone in it, that Inez's experience had tended to deny. She had spent her childhood immersed in the local conviction that the comfortable entrepreneurial life of an American colony in a tropic without rot represented a record of individual triumphs over a hostile environment. She had spent her adult life immersed in Harry Victor's conviction that he could be president.

This period in Hong Kong during which Inez ceased to claim the American exemption was defined by no special revelation, no instant of epiphany, no dramatic event. She had arrived in Hong Kong on the first day of April and she left it on the first day of May. During those four or five weeks mention of Janet and of Wendell Omura and of Janet's lanai gradually dropped out of even the Honolulu *Advertiser*, discarded copies of which Inez occasionally found in the lobbies of hotels frequented by flight crews.

Paul Christian was found incompetent to stand trial.

Adlai's vigil for the liberation of Saigon was edited into a vigil for "peace in Asia" and commended by the governor of Massachusetts as an instance of responsible campus expression, another situation managed by Billy Dillon.

The combat-loaded C-141 onto which Jack Lovett finally shoved Jessie (literally shoved, put his hands on her shoulders and pushed her through the hatch, because somewhere between Gate One and the loading ramp at Tan Son Nhut that evening Jessie realized that the flight Jack Lovett had told her they were meeting was her own, and tried to bolt) landed without incident at Agana, Guam, as did the commercial 747 on which Jessie sulked from Agana to Los Angeles.

Harry Victor met Jessie in customs.

He and Jessie had dinner at Chasen's.

Inez knew that Harry and Jessie had dinner at Chasen's because they called her in Hong Kong from their table, the front banquette inside the door. Jessie said that Jack Lovett had tricked her into going with him to Tan Son Nhut by saying that after he met this one flight they would go see the John Wayne movie playing at the Eden. Jessie said that she had not wanted to see the John Wayne movie in the first place but B.J. had gone back to the DAO after dinner which left nothing to do but see the John Wayne movie or sit there alone getting schitzy.

Jessie said that when she saw what was going down she asked Jack Lovett why she had to go on this flight and Jack Lovett had been rude.

Because I just shelled out a million piastres so you could, the fucker had said, and pushed her.

Hard.

She still had a bruise on her arm.

Forty-eight hours later.

"Tell the fucker I owe him a million piastres," Harry said when he came on the phone.

According to Inez Jessie landed in Los Angeles on the fifteenth of April.

According to Inez it was the twenty-eighth when she found she could no longer call Saigon; the twenty-ninth when American Service Radio in Saigon played "I'm Dreaming of a White Christmas" twice, played "The Stars and Stripes Forever" more times than Inez had counted, and stopped transmitting; and the first of May when Jack Lovett called her from Subic Bay and told her to meet him in Manila.

At one point I tried to work out a chronology for what Inez remembered of this period, and made the chart that still hangs on my office wall. The accuracy of this chart is problematic, not only because Inez kept no record of events as they happened but also because of the date line.

For example I have no idea whether Inez meant that the day Jessie landed in Los Angeles was the fifteenth in Los Angeles or the fifteenth in Hong Kong.

In either case the fifteenth seems doubtful, because Jack Lovett had been with Jessie in Saigon forty-eight hours before, promising her a John Wayne movie and bruising her arm, and many people believe Jack Lovett to have been in Phnom Penh for a period of some days (more than one day but fewer than five) between the time the American embassy closed there on the twelfth and the time the Khmer Rouge entered the city on the seventeenth. The report placing Jack Lovett in Phnom Penh after the embassy closed was one of the things that caused the speculation later, and eventually the investigation.

2

WHEN novelists speak of the unpredictability of human behavior they usually mean not unpredictability at all but a higher predictability, a more complex pattern discernible only after the fact. Examine the picture. Find the beast in the jungle, the figure in the carpet.

Context clues.

The reason why.

I have been examining this picture for some years now and still lack the reason why Inez Victor finally agreed to talk about what she "believed" had happened ("I believe we were in Jakarta," Inez would say, or "let's say it was May," as if even the most straightforward details of place and date were intrinsically unknowable, open to various readings) during the spring and summer of 1975.

At first she did not agree.

At first I talked to Billy Dillon and to Harry Victor and to Dwight Christian and even briefly to Jessie and to Adlai and to Dick Ziegler, each of whom, as I have suggested, had at least a limited stake in his or her own version of events, but Inez remained inaccessible. In the first place the very fact of where she and Jack Lovett seemed to be ruled out any pretense of casual access. I could call Dwight Christian and say that I just happened to be in Honolulu, but I could not call Inez and say that I just happened to be in Kuala Lumpur. No one "happens to be" in Kuala Lumpur, no one "passes through" en route somewhere else: Kuala Lumpur is en route nowhere, and for me to see Inez there implied premeditation, a definite purpose on my part and a definite decision on hers.

In the second place Inez seemed, that summer and fall after she left Honolulu with Jack Lovett, emotionally inaccessible. She seemed to have renounced whatever stake in the story she might have had, and erected the baffle of her achieved serenity between herself and what had happened. *It's the summer monsoon and quite sticky, you don't want to visit during the monsoon really but I'm sure Harry and Billy between them can sort out what you need to know. Excuse haste. Regards, Inez V.*

This was the response, scrawled on a postcard showing the lobby of the Hotel Equatorial in Kuala Lumpur, to the letter I wrote from Honolulu in July of 1975 asking Inez if she would see me. Since the "summer monsoon" in Kuala Lumpur is followed immediately by the "winter monsoon," which in turn lasts until the onset of the next "summer monsoon," Inez's response was even less equivocal than it might seem. In October, from Los Angeles, I wrote a second letter, and more or less promptly received a second postcard, again showing the lobby of the Hotel Equatorial, where incidentally Inez was not staying: *What you mention is all in the past and frankly I'd rather look ahead. In other words a visit would be unproductive. I.*

This card was postmarked the second of November and arrived in Los Angeles the fifteenth. Ten days later I received a third communication from Inez, a clipping of a book review, in which my name was mentioned in passing, from a month-old *International Herald-Tribune.* The note stapled to the clipping read *Sorry if my note seemed abrupt but you see my point I'm sure, Inez.* It was one week after that when Inez called my house in Los Angeles, having gone to some lengths to get the number, and asked me to come to Kuala Lumpur.

Actually she did not exactly "ask" me to come to Kuala Lumpur.

"When are you coming to K.L.," was what she said exactly.

I considered this.

"I wouldn't want to miss you," she said. "I could show you around."

At the time I thought that she had decided to talk to me only because Jack Lovett's name was just beginning to leak out of the various investigations into arms and currency and technology dealings on the part of certain former or perhaps even current overt and covert agents of the United States government. There had even been hints about narcotics dealings, which, although they made good copy and were played large in the early coverage (I recall the phrase

"Golden Triangle" in many headlines, and a photograph of two blurred figures leaving a house on Victoria Peak, one identified as a "sometime Lovett business associate" and the other as a "known Hong Kong Triad opium lord"), remained just that, hints, rumors that would never be substantiated, but the other allegations were solid enough, and not actually surprising to anyone who had bothered to think about what Jack Lovett was doing in that part of the world.

There had been the affiliations with interlocking transport and air courier companies devoid of real assets. There had been the directorship of the bank in Vila that put the peculiarities of condominium government to such creative use. There had been all the special assignments and the special consultancies and the special relationships in a fluid world where the collection of information was indistinguishable from the use of information and where national and private interests (the interests of state and non-state actors, Jack Lovett would have said) did not collide but merged into a single pool of exchanged favors.

In order to understand what Jack Lovett did it was necessary only to understand how natural it was for him to do it, how at once entirely absorbing and supremely easy. There had always been that talent for putting the right people together, the right man at the Department of Defense, say, with the right man at Livermore or Los Alamos or Brookhaven, or, a more specific example with a more immediately calculable payout, the Director of Base Development for CINC-PAC/MACV with Dwight Christian.

There had always been something else as well.

There had been that emotional solitude, a detachment that extended to questions of national or political loyalty.

It would be inaccurate to call Jack Lovett disloyal, although I suppose some people did at the time.

It would be accurate only to say that he regarded the country on whose passport he traveled as an abstraction, a state actor, one of several to be factored into any given play.

In other words.

What Jack Lovett did was never black or white, and in the long run may even have been (since the principal gain to him was another abstraction, the pyramiding of further information) devoid of ethical content altogether, but since shades of gray tended not to reproduce in the newspapers the story was not looking good on a breaking basis. That Jack Lovett had reportedly made some elusive deals with the failed third force (or fourth force, or fifth force, this was a story on which the bottom kept dropping out) in Phnom Penh in those days after the embassy closed there did not look good. That the London dealer who was selling American arms abandoned in South Vietnam had received delivery from one of Jack Lovett's cargo services did not look good. It seemed clear to me that the connection with Inez would surface quite soon (as it did, the week I came back from Kuala Lumpur, when the WNBC tape of Inez dancing with Harry Victor on the St. Regis Roof temporarily obliterated my actual memory of Inez), and I assumed that

Inez wanted to see me only because Jack Lovett wanted to see me. I assumed that Jack Lovett would find during my visit a way of putting out his own information. I assumed that Inez was acting for him.

In short I thought I was going to Kuala Lumpur as part of a defensive strategy that Inez might or might not understand.

This was, it turned out, too easy a reading of Inez Victor.

3

O N E thing she wanted to tell me was that Jack Lovett was dead.

That Jack Lovett had died on the nineteenth of August at approximately eleven o'clock in the evening in the shallow end of the fifty-meter swimming pool at the Hotel Borobudur in Jakarta.

After swimming his usual thirty laps.

That she had taken Jack Lovett's body to Honolulu and buried it on the twenty-first of August in the little graveyard at Schofield Barracks. Past where they buried the stillborn dependents. Beyond the Italian prisoners of war. Near a jacaranda tree, but the jacaranda had been out of bloom. When the jacaranda came into bloom and dropped its petals on the grass the pool of blue would just reach Jack Lovett's headstone. The grave was that close to the jacaranda. The colonel who had been her contact at Schofield had at first suggested another site but he had understood her objection. The colonel who had been her contact at Schofield had been extremely helpful.

Extremely cooperative.

Extremely kind really.

As had her original contact.

Mr. Soebadio. In Jakarta. Mr. Soebadio was the

representative for Java of the bank in Vila and it turned out to be his telephone number that Jack Lovett had given her to call if any problem arose during the four or five days they were to be in Jakarta.

Jack Lovett had not given her Mr. Soebadio's name. Only this telephone number.

To call. In case she was ill, or needed to reach him during the day, or he was in Solo or Surabaya and the rioting flared up again. In fact she had been thinking about this telephone number at the precise instant when she looked up and saw that Jack Lovett was lying face down in the very shallow end of the pool, the long stretch where the water was less than a foot deep and the little children with the Texas accents played all day.

It had been quite sudden.

She had watched him swimming toward the shallow end of the pool.

She had reached down to get him a towel.

She had thought at the exact moment of reaching for the towel about the telephone number he had given her, and wondered who would answer if she called it.

And then she had looked up.

There had been no one else at the pool that late. The last players had left the tennis courts, and the night lights had been turned off. Even the pool bar was shuttered, but there was a telephone on the outside wall, and it was from this telephone, twenty minutes later, that Inez called the number Jack Lovett had given her. She had sat on the edge of the pool with Jack Lovett's head in her lap until the Tamil doctor arrived. The Tamil doctor said that the twenty minutes she had spent giving Jack Lovett CPR had been beside the point. The Tamil doctor said that what happened had been instantaneous, circulatory, final. In the blood, he said, and simultaneously snapped his fingers and drew them across his throat, a short chop.

It was Mr. Soebadio who had brought the Tamil doctor to the pool.

It was Mr. Soebadio who worked Jack Lovett's arms into his seersucker jacket and carried him to the service area where his car was parked.

It was Mr. Soebadio who advised Inez to tell anyone who approached the car that Mr. Lovett was drunk and it was Mr. Soebadio who went back upstairs for her passport and it was Mr. Soebadio who suggested that certain possible difficulties in getting Mr. Lovett out of Indonesia could be circumvented by obtaining a small aircraft, what he called a good aircraft for clearance, which he happened to know how to do. He happened to know that there was a good aircraft for clearance on its way from Denpasar to Halim. He happened to know that the pilot, a good friend, would be willing to take Mrs. Victor and Mr. Lovett wherever Mrs. Victor wanted to go.

Within the limits imposed by the aircraft's range of course.

The aircraft being a seven-passenger Lear.

Halim to Manila, no problem.

Manila to Guam, no problem.

223

Honolulu, a definite problem, but with permission to refuel on certain atolls unavailable to commercial aircraft Mr. Soebadio believed that he could solve it.

Say Kwajalein.

Say Johnston.

Guam to Kwajalein, thirteen hundred miles approximately, well within range.

Kwajalein to Johnston, say eighteen hundred, adjust for drag since the prevailing winds were westward, still within range.

Johnston to Honolulu, seven hundred seventeen precisely and no problem whatsoever.

Mr. Soebadio had a pocket calculator and he stood on the tarmac at Halim working out the ratios for weight and lift and ground distance and wind velocity while Inez watched the Tamil doctor and the pilot lift Jack Lovett onto the back passenger seats in the Lear and get him into a body bag. Before he zipped the body bag closed the Tamil doctor went through the pockets of Jack Lovett's seersucker jacket and handed the few cards he found to Mr. Soebadio. Mr. Soebadio glanced at the cards and dropped them into his own pocket, still intent on his calculator. Inez considered asking Mr. Soebadio for whatever had been in Jack Lovett's pockets but decided against it. Somebody dies, you'd just as soon he didn't have your card in his pocket, Jack Lovett had told her once. The zipper on the body bag caught on the lapel of the seersucker jacket and Mr. Soebadio helped the Tamil doctor work it loose. Another thing Inez decided not to ask Mr. Soebadio was where the body bag had come from.

The cotton dress she was wearing was soaked with pool water and cool against her skin.

She smelled the chlorine all night long.

At Manila she did not get out of the Lear.

At Guam she was half asleep but aware of the descent and the landing strobes and the American voices of the ground crew. The pilot checked into the operations room and brought back containers of coffee and a newspaper. WHERE AMERICA'S DAY BEGINS, the newspaper had worked into the eagle on its flag.

At Kwajalein she could see the missile emplacements from the air and was told on the ground that she did not have clearance to get out of the plane.

At Johnston she did get out, and walked by herself to the end of the long empty runway, where the asphalt met the lagoon. Jack Lovett had spent three weeks on Johnston. 1952. Waiting on the weather. Wonder Woman Two was the name of the shot. She remembered that. She even remembered him telling her he had been in Manila, and the souvenir he brought. A Filipino blouse. Starched white lace. The first summer she was married to Harry she had found it in a drawer and worn it at Rehoboth. The starched white lace against her bare skin had aroused both of them and later Harry had asked why she never wore the blouse again.

Souvenir of Manila.

Bought on Johnston from a reconnaissance pilot who had flown in from Clark.

She knew now.

She took off her sandals and waded into the lagoon and splashed the warm water on her face and soaked her bandana and then turned around and walked back to the Lear. While the pilot was talking to the mechanics about a minor circuit he believed to be malfunctioning Inez opened the body bag. She had intended to place the wet bandana in Jack Lovett's hands but when she saw that rigor had set in she closed the body bag again. She left the bandana inside. Souvenir of Johnston. It occurred to her that Johnston would have been the right place to bury him but no one on Johnston had been told about the body on the Lear and the arrangement had already been made between Mr. Soebadio and the colonel at Schofield and so she went on, and did it at Schofield.

Which was fine.

Johnston would have been the right place but Schofield was fine.

Once she got the other site.

The site near the jacaranda.

The first site the colonel had suggested had been too near the hedge. The hedge that concealed the graves of the executed soldiers. There were seven of them. To indicate that they died in disgrace they were buried facing away from the flag, behind the hedge. She happened to know about the hedge because Jack Lovett had shown it to her, not long after they met. In fact they had argued about it. She had thought it cruel and unusual to brand the dead. Forever and ever. He had thought that it was not cruel and unusual at all, that it was merely pointless. That it was sentimental to think it mattered which side of the hedge they buried you on.

She remembered exactly what he had said.

The sun still rises and you still don't see it, he had said.

Nevertheless.

All things being equal she did not want him buried anywhere near the hedge and the colonel had seen her point right away.

So it had worked out.

It had all been fine.

She had taken a commercial flight to Singapore that night and changed directly for Kuala Lumpur.

She had called no one.

We were sitting after dinner on the porch of the bungalow Inez was renting in Kuala Lumpur when she told me this. It was my first day there. All afternoon at the clinic she had talked about Harry Victor and the Alliance for Democratic Institutions, and when I asked at dinner where Jack Lovett was she had said only that he was not in Kuala Lumpur. After dinner we had sat on the porch without speaking for a while and then she had begun, abruptly.

"Something happened in August," she had said.

Somewhere between Guam and Kwajalein she had asked if I wanted tea, and had brought it out to the porch in a chipped teapot painted with a cartoon that suggested the bungalow's period: a cigar-smoking

bulldog flanked by two rosebuds, one labeled "Lilli-
bet" and the other "Margaret Rose." Inez was barefoot. Her hair was pulled back and she was wearing
no makeup. There had been during the course of her
account a sudden hard fall of rain, temporarily walling
the porch with glassy sheets of water, and now after
the rain termites swarmed around the light and
dropped in our teacups, but Inez made no more note
of the termites than she had of the rain or for that
matter of the teapot. After she stopped talking we sat
in silence a moment and then Inez poured me another cup of tea and flicked the termites from its
surface with her fingernail. "What do you think
about this," she said.

I said nothing.

Inez was watching me closely.

I thought about this precisely what Inez must have
thought about this, but it was irrelevant. I thought
there had been papers shredded all over the Pacific the
night she was flying Jack Lovett's body from Jakarta
to Schofield, but it was irrelevant. We were sitting in
a swamp forest on the edge of Asia in a city that had
barely existed a century before and existed now only
as the flotsam of some territorial imperative and a
woman who had once thought of living in the White
House was flicking termites from her teacup and telling me about landing on a series of coral atolls in a
seven-passenger plane with a man in a body bag.

An American in a body bag.

An American who, it was being said, had been doing business in situations where there were not supposed to be any Americans.

What did I think about this.

Finally I shrugged.

Inez watched me a moment longer, then shrugged herself.

"Anyway we were together," she said. "We were together all our lives. If you count thinking about it."

Inside the bungalow the telephone was ringing.

Inez made no move to answer it.

Instead she stood up and leaned on the wooden porch railing and looked out into the wet tangle of liana and casuarina that surrounded the bungalow. Through the growth I could see occasional headlight beams from the cars on Ampang Road. If I stood I could see the lights of the Hilton on the hill. The telephone had stopped ringing before Inez spoke again.

"Not that it matters," she said then. "I mean the sun still rises and he still won't see it. That was Harry calling."

4

JACK Lovett had caught lobsters in the lagoon off Johnston in 1952. Inez had soaked her bandana in the lagoon off Johnston in 1975. Jessie and Adlai had played Marco Polo in the fifty-meter pool at the Borobudur in Jakarta in 1969. Jack Lovett had died in the fifty-meter pool at the Borobudur in Jakarta in 1975. In 1952 Inez and Jack Lovett had walked in the graveyard at Schofield Barracks. He had shown her the graves of the stillborn dependents, the Italian prisoners of war. He had shown her the hedge and the graves that faced away from the flag. The stillborn dependents and the Italian prisoners of war and the executed soldiers had all been there in 1952. Even the jacaranda would have been there in 1952.

During the five days I spent in Kuala Lumpur Inez mentioned such "correspondences," her word, a number of times, as if they were messages intended specifically for her, evidence of a narrative she had not suspected. She seemed to find these tenuous connections extraordinary. Given a life in which the major cost was memory I suppose they were.

By the time I got back to Los Angeles a congressional subpoena had been issued for Jack Lovett and the clip of Inez dancing on the St. Regis Roof had made its first network appearance. I have no idea why this particular clip was the single most repeated image of a life as exhaustively documented as Inez Victor's, but it was, and over those few days in January of 1976 this tape took on a life quite independent of the rather unexceptional moment it recorded, sometimes running for only a second or two, cut so short that it might have been only a still photograph; other times presenting itself as an extended playlet, reaching a dramatic curtain as the aide said "Hold two elevators" and Harry Victor said "I'm just a private citizen" and Inez said "Marvelous" and the band played "Isn't It Romantic."

I suppose one reason the tape was played again and again was simply that it remained the most recent film available on Inez Victor.

I suspect another reason was that the hat with the red cherries and "Just a private citizen" and "Marvelous" and "Isn't It Romantic" offered an irony accessible to even the most literal viewer.

Three weeks later a Washington *Post* reporter happened to discover in the Pentagon bureau of records that the reason Jack Lovett had not answered his congressional subpoena was that he had been dead since August, buried in fact on government property, and that the signature on the government forms authorizing his burial on government property was Inez Victor's.

That night the tape ran twice more, and then not again.

At any rate not again that I knew about, not even when NBC located Inez Victor at the refugee administration office in Kuala Lumpur and Inez Victor declined to be interviewed.

In March of 1976 Billy Dillon showed me the thirteen-word reply he got to a letter he had written Inez. He had resorted to writing the letter because calling Inez had been, he said, unsatisfactory.

"Raise anything substantive on the telephone," Billy Dillon said when he showed me Inez's reply, "Mother Teresa out there says she's wanted in the clinic. So I write. I give her the news, a little gossip, a long thought or two, I slip in one question. One. I ask if she can give me one fucking reason she's in goddamn K.L., and this is what I get. Thirteen words."

He handed me the sheet of lined paper on which, in Inez's characteristic scrawl, the thirteen words appeared: *"Colors, moisture, heat, enough blue in the air. Four fucking reasons. Love, Inez."*

Colors, moisture, heat.
Enough blue in the air.
I told you the essence of that early on but not the context, which has been, you will note, the way I tried to stay on the wire in this novel of fitful glimpses. It has not been the novel I set out to write, nor am I exactly the person who set out to write it. Nor have I experienced the rush of narrative inevitability that

usually propels a novel toward its end, the momentum that sets in as events overtake their shadows and the cards all fall in on one another and the options decrease to zero.

Perhaps because nothing in this situation encourages the basic narrative assumption, which is that the past is prologue to the present, the options remain open here.

Anything could happen.

As you may or may not know Billy Dillon has a new candidate, a congressman out of NASA who believes that his age and training put him on the right side of what he calls "the idea lag," and occasionally when Billy Dillon is in California to raise money I have dinner with him. In some ways I have replaced Inez as the woman Billy Dillon imagines he wishes he had married. Again as you may or may not know Harry Victor is in Brussels, special envoy to the Common Market. Adlai and Jessie are both well, Adlai in San Francisco, where he clerks for a federal judge on the Ninth Circuit; Jessie in Mexico City, where she is, curiously enough, writing a novel, and living with a *Newsweek* stringer who is trying to log in enough time in various troubled capitals to come back to New York and go on staff. When and if he does I suspect that Jessie will not come up with him, since her weakness is for troubled capitals. *Imagine my mother dancing,* I had hoped that Jessie's novel would begin, but according to a recent letter I had from her this particular novel is an historical romance about Maximilian and Carlota.

Inez of course is still in Kuala Lumpur.

She writes once a week to Jessie, somewhat less often to Adlai, and scarcely at all now to Harry. She sends an occasional postcard to Billy Dillon, and the odd clipping to me. One evening a week she teaches a course in American literature at the University of Malaysia and has dinner afterwards at the Lake Club, but most of her evenings as well as her days are spent on the administration of what are by now the dozen refugee camps around Kuala Lumpur.

A year ago when I was in London the *Guardian* ran a piece about Southeast Asian refugees, and Inez was quoted.

She said that although she still considered herself an American national (an odd locution, but there it was) she would be in Kuala Lumpur until the last refugee was dispatched.

Since Kuala Lumpur is not likely to dispatch its last refugee in Inez's or my lifetime I would guess she means to stay on, but I have been surprised before. When I read this piece in London I had a sudden sense of Inez and of the office in the camp and of how it feels to fly into that part of the world, of the dense greens and translucent blues and the shallows where islands once were, but so far I have not been back.